I0738493

ANTIQUARY

poems and stories

ANTIQUARY

poems and stories

Peter Weltner

For Robert Mohr and Atticus Carr
and
To the Memory of Linda Gregg

Table of Contents

IV.

I.

Pilgrim

A pilgrim wearing a mourning cloak,
traveling in a boat with a single sail
as it glides on the Galilee. Dawn winds
rustle the rushes by the shore.

The blunted bulk of an ox heaves
itself awake. A thirsty ram bounds
from rock to rock searching
for shade, licking the dew off stones.

Lizards and snakes slither through sand
to hide from the heat. Hermit-hived,
honey-headed bees swarm in search of pollen.
The sea sleeps peaceful as a newborn in its bed.

Repairing nets, their skiffs tied by rope to poles,
fishermen wade in up to their thighs.
Locusts rattle like palms
wind-tossed by a gathering storm.

Will the head-high reeds divide,
the desert bear fruit for those
brought here by hard bought journeys,
dreamers seeking a lost oasis?

This is my despair, the old man thinks,
his face both sad and solemn,
the heart's desolation, the clarity
of empty places, Adonai's all-seeing eye.

Wrens, waxwings, thrushes sing
of deep things, the sea scorched
by the fires burning heaven
from a sun like Elijah flying skyward and free.

Grieve, my friend, for the temple that has fallen
inside you, the tears, the lament
through the twice thousand years wait
of Jerusalem's sons and daughters.

Symphony of Sorrowful Songs, Sung by Ewa Izykowska

Imagine yourself
in Athens
at the Theater of Dionysos
during the spring
or fall festival
in the fifth century
before Christ
at a performance
of Antigonae
while she chants
her last speech,
her threnody to life.
Think of yourself
at a rite like that,
what it means
for your time,
your city and its people.

September, 1939

A land like a man and his sons trapped, coiled
by snakes attacking from the holes
they slithered out of,
the wet-hemp-rope-like
noose of serpents

the soldiers invading, strangling us
from the east, west,
marching through forests,
down mountains,
across plains and valleys,

the terror of being suffocated
women, men,
children wailing, dying
in barns, houses, cities,
their ancient walls and towers in flames,

struggling to free themselves
from the scaly knots shackling
their lives,
heaving a cry, bellowing like a bull
as their country is led to the altar,

cowering below soldiers' axes
and hammers,
under guns, tanks, bombs,
blaming the gods, the silent,
indifferent gods,

cursing the fate ensnaring them,
the clutch of monsters
crushing them, a country

smothered,
asphyxiated,
like a man, a priest

who saw too clearly,
who dared to warn
of the trick of the horse
and was not believed.

His Son, My Father

1.

My father and two uncles fought in France
where I fight a generation after them.
My brother is a p.o.w. in New Guinea.
A smart-assed cousin spies for the OSS.

In a week or two, no longer, my best mate
will be out of hospital minus an arm.
Da sits in his overstuffed chair
in our cramped flat in the East End.

He orders his wife, my widowed sister
to dress always in black as they knit
socks, sweaters, warm caps for soldiers.
Mornings, he drinks tea, reads the papers.

Afternoons, he listens to dispatches
on the wireless. Nights, he scans
the skies for German planes until
the Thames, kindled by dawn, glows rosy.

We've always been Londoners, city
smart and cocky. Da watches
the fires. A phantom. War-maddened
by poisonous fog, the guns it hides.

Wanders through the smoke, picking bits
of glass, cracked crockery, ribbons,
soggy books, a medal or two out of
the rubble and ash. Saves what he can.

6

Ignoring flares, incendiaries, barrages,
he's slogging in Passchendaele's mud
hunting for comrades the fucking Huns
left half buried, mired in muck and sludge.

2.

Listen. The guns across the river keep
shooting. The jerries are re-grouping
in woods. I didn't mean to leave you.
I'm told the war is over. But I hear guns.

Our platoon has drawn enemy attention.
Yesterday, they shot Tom. Death is our gift
for the birthday of time. I love the sun and stars.
I miss the easiness of bed and slumber.

This war. That war. This battle. That
battle. This one. That one. This
that. This that. What's that? Clock
on our mantlepiece ticking away ticking.

All night under the stars, less white
than here. I give thanks for beer,
rum, dark red grenadine. Praise
days of a birth with no hedgerows.

Chatter of coal and logs by fires. Raising
a pint in a pub. Romance would have
happened if I had had less courage,
the afterward life of an iron-sheathed heart.

7

On the eleventh of November I sent you
a tender sign of fall, a shadow from
a shattered tree outside my trench.
Don't hide your face. Don't turn away in anger.

Dress in fine clothes, my sons, be hopeful.
I bear news that will make humanity
rejoice. The peace to come will set
us free. No war can last forever.

3.

Troop ships no longer dock on the Thames to transport
soldiers to France. Rotting piers' pilings rise
out of mist. The river needs dredging. It's a short
boat ride east across the channel to the cemeteries.
See the lies dead moons shine on dead men's faces,
their eyes white as a blind man's. Why do you still wait
to learn of our fate? Verey lights. Flares' traces.
And Johnny in their glare. My best friend. My mate.
Bone dumps. The curse of mud. Sun-glow on quarries.
A pier is a bridge to nowhere. Don't leave. Late
to the peace, I'm sailing home. If you can't sleep, dive
into my dreams. Try to meet me there. I've heard rumors
of better worlds. Time to clear the seashore. Wars
never end. Trawl the harbor. Find me. Tell me if I'm still alive.

At the War Memorial

"Captured at the Yalu River," his wife said. "A hundred
men killed. Dressed for summer, the rest marching
to the prison camps. Lots froze. Or were half-dead
from starvation, their wounds. The Chinese did nothing
to save them. Passed them on to the North Koreans
who put them in pits to be eaten alive by rats.
Tied them to tripods. Soaked them with water. Man's
a wolf to man all right. Most froze. Worse than combat
those camps' torments, I'm told. Thousands died.
From dysentery. Malnutrition." A rage that's survived
her husband's suffering, trying to describe the unspeakable
years after she had learned the truth. She holds a Bible
in her hand. "Why do we do this to each other? Why?"
She grabs the sleeve of my jacket. "Tell me. Please. You. Anybody."

Whitman's War

The war is nearly over, but the hospitals are even fuller
than before. Most wounds are in the legs and arms,
but there is every kind of wound–little can deter
a minié ball or bullet–in every part–what harms
can be inflicted on a man–of the body. Typhoid fever.
Diarrhoea. Cartarrahl afflictions. Bronchitis. Pneumonia.
He waits tonight by the bedside–he'd crossed the river,
seen death in his face–of a new arrival. He is a
brother, father, mother, lover who grasps his hands.
He soothes his pain. He always kisses him. Will see
how in a nearby ward his brother is doing. Walt stands
over them and touches them. One is a Unionist, Army
of the Potomac. The other Secesh. In one battle
both were hit. Each ever dying inside him. Yankee. Rebel.

Ward 5B

She is a young nurse, a shy novice frightened of
Ward 5B, the men, boys in it not much older
than she is. A few are younger. Rushed doctors shove
her aside when she is in their way. She drinks water
from the cooler, reads a chart, fixes her cap,
knocks before she walks in. Sometimes he's shit
himself or vomited blood. The room stinks. On his lap
waits a tray of uneaten food. His sunken eyes are lit
by fear, like a skunk's or raccoon's in the dark
behind her apartment. For the first time, she risks it.
She touches his forehead, tries to soothe him, remarks
how his fever has gone down, comments on how the cit-
y is beautiful today, the weather fine. Oh, the sky's
so blue today. So lovely. He cries. And she cries. And lies and lies.

Gods, after Hölderlin

1.

Holy Socrates, why do you ceaselessly give yourself
  to that young man. Are you not concerned with
    loftier matters? Why do you stare at him
      so longingly, with the love owed to gods?

Those who think most profoundly love what's most vital.
  Those who see the world clearly admire youth's splendor.
    Those who are wisest will, at last,
      worship whatever is most beautiful.

2.

Saċred realm of the Greeks, home to the gods,
  Is it true, what youth taught us?
Hall of feasts, its floor the sea whose tables are mountains
  built in a holier time to fulfill a great need!
But where are the thrones, where the temples, their vessels?
  Where the songs that please the gods like nectar?
Where, oh where do they shine, the oracular truths?
  Delphi slumbers. Where now does tragedy sing?
Where is quickness? Where does one see omnipotent joy
  break out of the sky to dazzle eyes, ravage ears with thunder?
Father Aether! Someone cried and voice after voice took up
  the chant a thousand times and more. Who can bear life alone?
Shared fortune proffers joy. And, later, with strangers exchanged,
  it yields an exultation, words, words as exalted as sleep.
Father! Oh mind-piercing clarities. How far they travel. An an-
cient
  sign passed down, now distant, yet striking, penetrating, creating
what paradise has given. As heaven enters, its presence shakes the
earth
  awake from its shadows and man from his gloom strides into Day.

3.

Their quieted hearts were filled with a silent contentment
  and, as from the beginning, alone, desire was satisfied.
Such is man, if fortune is true and he is granted its gifts
  by a god, though he sees and understands none of it.
First he must suffer. For now he names the beloved things.
  Now he must pursue the words that bud and blossom like flowers.

Eternity, after Rimbaud

Discovered again.
What? Eternity,
the light of the sun
become sea.

Watchman of the soul,
never tire
of quietly saying, Night is nothing,
the day on fire.

From the world's approval,
from vulgar high-
spirits, remove
yourself, freely fly.

Then from you alone,
you, your glowing satin ashes,
duty breathes easily, though stone
silent. No one says, No more.

There's no hope. All's done.
No 'orietur.' Nothing stirs. Nothing rises.
Knowledge comes from patience.
No suffering you feel, no pain surprises.

Recovered, renewed again.
What is? Eternity.
The light of the sun
becomes sea.

Nietzsche in Turin

Stop abusing that horse. I order you.
Cease whipping it. Cruelty
is maddening. Why do
you beat it? Pity
the poor creature. Its back
bleeds. Its hairless haunches
are peeling skin. Quit attack-
ing it. What wretches
men are. Look at me. I have no friends. Music
pleases me no more. I can't dance.
My spirit is sick.
What ill-gotten fod-
der have you been feeding it? The hideous trance
life is, the lies it tells. And I, Dionysos, its god,

a boulder in a river, the heights of a mountain,
a tiger raging, a leopard preying, a sleeping lion,
a man who knows no pain
he can't reign over. A man of passion,
not bastardly Wagner,
that priest-demented fool of a Parsifal.
Wine, delight best cater
to my tastes. Symposia. Feasts. Call
me a tragic Greek unashamed of life.
Undaunted. Proud. Indomitable. And you, you appall-
ing man, I demand you stop. Yes. Truth is strife,
conflict, combat, war. The eternal
recurrence of the same. But the beast, that poor beaten
beast. And I, Dionysos, helpless, a god among men.

Ravel

Monet's Argenteuil, the Seine
flowing below a bridge, clouds' shadows,
birds singing in trees,
salmon upstream, a Paris-
ian sky, silvery minnows
sparkling through reeds. A barge tows
two skiffs. The light is Grecian.
In nearby woods, dryads dance to Pan,
bewitched by joy,
cockerels at sunrise–
he, too, bewildered by spring's
hellenic radiance, to be forever a boy
dreaming under crystalline skies,
a pagan child in an age of endless mornings.

                              He blesses
his killers as he climbs the gallows' stairs, so long
imprisoned, years silenced, protestor, plotter against history's
most evil tyranny, against its cruel laws. It is wrong
to murder. Yet he has taken that sin, glory's
ruin, upon himself. No, not a saint, not a martyr,
not a holy man, no, he would insist.

                         Religionless religion.
Enigmatic phrase he coined to stir
up debate, freedom of belief, a reason
to question all creeds, to think everything
newly, to return to the beginning.

What did he see or feel as the noose was placed
round his neck? What music, if any,
did he hear? Faced
by death, seconds left before he is murdered, did he see
God? The beatitudes
were all you needed, he had said. Was he blessed? Did he pray
for grace in the seconds before his end?

No one can say. Solitude's
what dying is. You, me, they
who read him later, are trying to comprehend,
to interpret, to understand what?

                         Religionless religion.
The son
in Mark's dark vision of his final moments on the cross,
abandoned by his father, forsaken,
cries out like a man in prison
who is guilty of no crime yet condemned to the loss

of his life and its light.

                    What if it was despair
he was silently confessing to?

What if it is your dying cry, the prayer
of your unwilling disbelief,
that in the end descends from heaven and blesses you?

II.

Reverence

1.

I want to say my village's park
was secluded as an island,
my backyard fence
a Spartan rampart my mother

watched me climb over. I want
to say the bruised elbow,
the skinned knee I washed
in the creek was cleansed in the Styx.

Grass tickles my toes. Cool water
trickles over my feet. Dandelions.
A warm wind, sifting through pines.
The forms of things mutating.

Tadpoles to frogs. Crayfish
under rocks. Sweet incense
of magnolia, roses, budding
leaves, honeysuckle.

A wall of twigs I build high as Troy's.
Each stone I throw hurled
with the power of a Cyclops.
Clouds like sails unfurled by Zephyrus.

Locusts' wild chirring enticing
as Sirens. A black horned beetle
fiercer than Ajax. Swallows
twirling in sorrow. I want to say

I was a child whose sun was the one
I read about in a book of Greek
stories. Gods. Apollo's hibiscus.
White-walnut thick-limbed as Zeus.

21

2.

High over my head, oak and poplar
leaves, pine needles let little
sunlight seep through to where
I play in woods' morning shadows.

The wet bark from a stand
of loblollies smells of wood smoke
and my father's workroom's
turpentine. Beneath my feet,

decaying leaves yield to
my weight as a yard-long snake
slithers through weeds
toward me. More out of fright,

I like to think, than meanness,
I throw a rock at it, scaring
it back toward the lake
where the moccasin swims away.

I pick at a phlegm colored clot
of sap, sniff it, chew it
like used gum, sharp and bitter.
I would taste it still, the flavor

of it lingering on my tongue
seventy years later,
the resinous, acrid
pungency in things a child

like a wild thing swallows. Cardinals, a jay.
A feral cat squabbling with robins.
Tadpoles, newts, minnows. A no
trespassing sign rotting along the trail.

Kudzu entangling trunks darker
weeds clasp tighter. Clouds, drained
and gauzy, drifting off, the air
left humid and fragrant. I crouch

on a wide flat rock, sip sweet water
from a spring. If I could rise
to paradise someday. Into sanctity.
Redbud. Dogwood. Deodar cedar.

3.

Old woods are where, a kid,
I hid from myself in the deepest
dark of a forest crushed
by vine and brush, the sky

wet as if it were perpetually
drizzling, pine, oak, hickory bark
black as duff, the thick
canopy diffusing sunlight

to a dusky bronze glow
or the shine off gold.
Go home, boy. The last light
fades. So woods say.

Or, if you must stay, hike deeper in.
Get more lost than you
have ever been before.
I would live in one clear place,

never a stranger, never
far from home, nothing
at the end deprived
of where I began long ago.

Or wander through twilight
miles out in the country,
far further in than the forest
lets me, choosing to lose my way,

unguided by sight, forgetting
the day, the things I
learned there, night
grasping me by my arm,

a light drizzle falling
through leaves,
holly, rhododendron,
fennel pale as green mist–

in the moonlight, the kind air,
the life I am leaving behind–
like an old friend hesitant
to follow–bidding goodbye.

4.

To be at The Cloisters again,
my mother holding my hand
as a sole solider strolls the walk

where she gazes
over the palisades,
silvery as the bridge's towers.

Inside, gold-threaded tapestries
faded to a comic book's colors,
crucifixes splintered,

Christ's face as pocked by worm holes
as attic beams in our old house.
My mother bows to a relic holder

or to the lost bones it once held
and displayed. Stained glass
paints her red and green.

In the garden, the air is herb scented.
We rest on a bench to listen
to monks chanting in the chapel.

She squeezes my hand. I must be
quiet. I turn six next week.
The voices rise and fall like arches.

My mother will die and so will I
and I don't want us to.
Like paradise, they sound.

A Land Believed to Be Eden

1.

Backyard woods, high grass, sumac, milkweed
to chop through, to play soldiers in,
erect pup tents
pitched on pine-needle-prickly packed red clay.

A biting November day, black beetles
lumbering under rocks,
dusky moss felt-soft on bark,
musty as a trunk in an attic packed with old things.

A dead wren, its feathers merging with the gray
mud on the banks of the creek.
Ants, a few white grubs,
milky caterpillars, foot-long blood-red worms.

A spider knits its web among dew-wet ferns
that glint in a shaft of sunlight.
Distant threads of clouds wind
upward, dissolving. Wild ivy, honeysuckle

threading in and out of brush, meshed tendrils
thick as a fat man's fingers.
Jagged pebbles, round slick
shiny stones scattered on a creek's shallow bed.

2.

Night, the stars off course, the sun in dreamtime
blackening. Five-toed frogs. Salamanders
big as hogs. Bleeding rocks.
Two headed dogs. Grotesqueries. Residues of daytime thoughts.

26

A pine tree cracking apart, smoldering,
split by lightning. Clouds, mist
blowing like veils on the horizon seen
through a shadowy light that got left behind deep into woods.

A creek rippling, leaves rustling in chilling breezes.
Cowbells past twilight. The upswell, downswell
of night creatures rustling, insects' buzzing.
The silvery gleam by the moon of moths

flapping their wings.
A snake blithely slithers toward water. The universe
longing to live forever. Starlight
seeping through oak, poplar, sycamore,
leaves pallid as grass when it's covered by a week-old snowfall.

The carcass of a beaver, its pelt the dappled gray
of mold. Remember me, the wren
you saw this morning, whenever you
dream of Eden. Remember me, child, when you grow old.

3.

The streets of Memphis are burning
from rage, rioters incited
by racist outsiders.
Tanks crush a revolt in Budapest, Prague.

Children no older than I am are dying
in Algeria, Egypt, China.
In a magazine I see bodies tangled
in barbed wire, loose bricks, charred posts, burnooses.

In the showers after gym, I try not to look
but can't help seeing. Every night,
I die from shame. Every night,
I make promises I know I won't keep.

Eden is the rite of atonement
commanded of Cain.
For his wrath, their pain.
The fish belly white of boys in the photographs.

I rake my father's lawn, whack a stick at caterpillar
tents, at webs threading through vines. Sap
clings to my skin, a resiny gum I scrub
off in the bathtub.   Clean as on the first day, I say. Clean as Adam.

Shoreline

Far out to sea, waves crash into each other,
breaking, cascading onto shore, their rage at water's edge a pent-
up force, a sort of protest. A plover
picks at a bed of kelp a stray dog sniffs warily.
Yesterday, I went
away from here for a while, scared of it all, escaped inside.
Waiting for the storms
of north county smoke to pass through,
hoping the ash-gray sea would be washed away
a new one open to the sky as a field of sunflowers
might, seeking light, anxious to bloom.

Waves break
and break again on the beach,
teaching us about
tragedy, how it repeats itself for the sake
of a rhythm not ours,
obedient to no human measure. Below
the seawall, a shrunken, grizzled man
huddles in a blanket he's found,
his hard life, years of sorrow
clear in his dust-crusted eyes.

He's heeding the shoreline
as if the ground
under his feet were shifting, where he stands
wayward, dangerous.
The air is chalky gray,
hard to breathe, thick
with smoke from ravaging wildfires north of the bay.
Gulls caw caw caw, ravens clack, pipers make their little click-
ing noises. What have men done
to the sun?
Long rainless days ever hotter, wilder.

Tired, the old man crouches
under his sand-blackened blanket.
Now,
the ember glow of late dawn seeps
through smoldering clouds.
Tomorrow,
the sun will rise
a fiery orange flashing bright as a signal light
intending to warn.

Showers of bone,
torrents of cinders scattering
over the sea as surfers watch
how the waves break,
oblivious to what's at stake,
downed cliffs
crumbling dunes
flattened highway
houses drowned
nothing here left
after disaster reclaims the world
we mistook for ours.

The World Was Made to Be a Scene of Love

A child, a child
            dreaming of loss, of being
                without parents,

abandoned, free, wants nothing
                more than to be who he is,
                        happy in the wild

places he lives in at night,
                        asleep, a bird on the wing
without belongings,

                        just seeing all the air brings
with the wind,
                like a sparrow or wren flying

freely. Night's wide starlit heavens,
                    the sky's clarity
                        on a cloudless day.

I remember, as a boy,
                using the wide lens
                        of a magnifying glass

and sun's rays on decay-
        ing leaves to make them burn,
                        the wind blow-

ing ashes into the sky
                where all things
                        a child sets on fire go.

All Worlds Being But a Silent Wilderness

Childhood can be a pagan time,
souls dwelling in stones, a forest
inhabited by spirits. So his life began and stayed
until he heard mournful tears
as eden departed from rocks and streams and lakes.

       Gods once lived inside
all things or else his childhood lied.

       Time itself fears change,
the harsh lessons the sea-
sons come to teach a boy once certain
he was immortal, not wanting to be
more today than he was yesterday, the cure
for any sorrows he might have known found in the bliss
of woods, the joy of being where nothing is miss-
ing,
the ten thousand lasting beauties of every wilderness.

Drink.
       The water here, this high in the mountains,
this far from roads, is free from pollution,
from fires' ashes, the air balmy,
fragrant with spruce, fir, rhododendron, late rains,
the sweetness of new leaves. The sun
is steady in the sky as if ordered by
the Lord not to move for a moment. The birds
are still as statues. No bushes rustle.

Be quiet.
               Try
to find in this silence your own stillness, the will-
lessness of creation.

Old man, lie down
and cry
for more worlds than this one.

33

Redwood

Bald trees, no limbs to climb, foliage gleaming in a shaded light,
as snow shadows day, while you try to see far away
though only what's near is clear, vision intensified by
exactitude, this leaf, that needle, bark scrap, naked trunk:
whatever's more precise than memory in the back of an eye.

Think of Barnett Newman's zips or Pollock's Blue Poles,
how you dance to the rhythm of what they envision.
Consciousness must betray itself to be free,
must trust the ghosts concealed in things outside it,
these redwoods half seen, though no less certain, in shades of gray.

How quiet the wilderness is today, wet from dew, the mist
that perpetually falls in woods, the murmur of a distant rain
that is part of what you know, is you, the light muted
by the moisture dribbling off redwoods, brush, and vines,
the music of a rainy morning's hushed musings, its silence broken.

Or perhaps this is noon, this burnished gray, blackened brightness,
not the sun's, but a gift of the primeval world you enter
with your camera: illusionless, stark, half-awake dreaming trees
as depicted on an ancient paper scroll, washed in watery ink, nature
painterly, the cold, fading light you'll sleep better by deep back in
  the forest.

A Screen, a Painting, a Bowl

1.

The screen is too wide to take it all in
in one view.
No matter how far back you stand,
the mountains,

like gigantic moss-covered
pine cones, lean,
look to be bent askew
by time and wind,

their slopes too sheer
to hike. Move
from panel to panel.
So much is shown

in miniature—minuscule cranes,
two men poling
two tiny boats
and a thin river slightly widening

as it flows west—that you think,
culture, a civilization,
tradition, means this:
life intensified, movement stilled.

2.

A solitary duck floats
downstream.
High up, in a wood hut,
two men,

in fluent robes, talk, gesturing,
their aged faces
little more than a few,
quick brush strokes.

In a den of sorts, not quite the mouth
of a cave, a monk sits,
praying, shaded by clouds
and a plum tree trunk.

3.

Turn around. A porcelain bowl
displayed in a case
behind thick glass,
is white like robes worn to mourn

a passed soul, pure
as a jade vase
vast age has not changed
save for a swirl

of pale blue around
a thin inner rim—
an almost flat pot,
or dish, silent as frost.

Some day it will come, like
a blunt moment
of shock, spirits appearing
while you sleep. A new

bowl, whiter than fresh snow
but old in its devotions,
a monk praying in a cave
the hands that moulded it.

III.

Freshman Convocation, September 1960

Sitting in the three story chapel,
  austere, protestant,
thin maroon velvet cushions
  on dark, hard pews,
white walls and columns, clear
  framed panes, sent
there by hope, I suppose,
  listening to news
of our new lives, two hundred
  boys and more,
learning the traditions, rules
  we'll have obeyed
or not before we leave while
  from outside, a door
of the chapel half open,
  the aureate light, unfaded,
of early fall pours in, the chill
  air, summer
over, we breathe in, not know-
  ing what will become
of us, strolling to our rooms in
  Dunham, the thrill
of debating the days ahead,
  what's in store, not yet sum-
  moned
by the first hints of autumn on
  the Hill
to be brought to bloom like
  trees with snow in a final
  winter.

Switzerland

1.

Sadness, a word rules say you can't start a poem with,
but do anyway. Sadness like smoke from
a smoldering fire
blowing downwind

to where I lie uneasily, waiting
for you. Like a sky in December
smudged a dark olive gray
or the charcoal of long-trodden slate

or the empty white my life looks like
behind the roiling clouds,
the blank, blanched white
that sadness exposes by the absence inside me

or the snowy trail of the ship
my eyes follow
drifting westward
until its wake sinks into an ice-capped sea.

2.

The sadness of the movie I watched last night,
how happiness eluded the characters in it.
In my dreams afterwards, a great gray monster
stomped down empty hallways,

pounding on doors, trying to reach
my bedroom or his, the Swiss boy in the film,
Mario, who like me came out too late,
his youth, his most ardent years

denied him, lost to disguises his need for praise required
and a rapturous secrecy. Sadness
not from a bad mistake or a defining failure, then,
but more the gray of a memory like a window

so cold you can write your name on it with a finger,
freezing rains streaming over gutters
in a storm that never quits,
the despair to come like the end of a year fast closing in.

3.

I am watching the movie again in my head and cannot change
how it ends. Love denied.
The sadness there is no pushing away, out of mind,
out of soul, no running from even if you wanted to leave it,

the satiation of mid-winter days never to be realized
or grasped, the whiteness you want
to last forever,
to lie in, to hide in, his ever present absence.

And you, Mario, like a snowfall
that blankets all,
the whole recumbent earth,
staying by me, embracing me,

the steady cold I seek from you,
the impassioned sadness,
the consoling sorrow
I learned from our lost boyhoods.

Saga

Born out of the North Sea, waves like horses'
haunches, their manes like whips,
its groundswell and surge, tidal barrage
of an island home, its only harbor lying lee-

ward. Storms, heavy rains
toss boats like buoys. It takes courage
to live there, wind-swept rocks, stark as a desert,
treeless, its mountainous desolations.

Who would stay here? You,
maybe, like a convert
to a bleaker new religion that shuns
all sensual pleasures. You, my Norseman, who

said I was fated to be, in the way of your homeland
  an arctic tern at sea
flying from pole to pole, I as ravenous as they,
  as insatiably hungry.

A Longship

Light as pure as Schubert's Nacht
und Träume sung by Elly Ameling,
   that "little Dutch girl"
Wustman called her, an icy brittle
   light, as if peering through
frosted glass you are shocked to discover
   how cold the sun can be,
how like snow the sky it terrorizes
   with its whiteness.
Tides, fresh or salty, flow into and out
   of the inlets of an island
at north's far horizon, the seas people
   go to die nearby
where maps grow silent, vision confounded
   by what it sees too keenly,
sun moon mountains clouds mist sand,
   glowing and raw.
Birds perch by water's edge, eager to fly
   wherever they please,
like souls preparing for night, the old light
   in its new boat setting sail,
Sol in his viking ship set on fire, the dead
   with their hoard
as it burns like dawn gifted with gold,
   oar-steered and steady.

Shetland

Rocks, many a black jagged promontory
   jutting into the sea,
shrouded, gauzy, the dun gray or muted blue
   of the sky. Few signs
of life. A crime may be either night or day
   or both, like a memory
you're trying to forget of someone
   you've loved and lost
or regret not having loved enough
   before nothing is left
of them but your grief. The island is bereft,
   empty in most places
like a chill in the evening that makes people
   shudder, like a will o wisp
glowing on an icy lake, felt without being seen.
   The earth has been stripped,
denuded to rocks, water, sky, their naked consolation.
   Is sorrow what it takes
to discover, if innocent, what guilt feels like?
   Rocks darker than midnight,
blacker than fears and trepidations. As if free,
   more stunning than sunlight,
the Shetlands rise out of the sea like breasts of massive
   matter. It is their right
that men should die while stones live on and on.
   The tides,
the wind-stricken beaches
   have no alibi
and yet if pressed refuse
   as you would
to confess, cold as the heart
   of a Nordic moon.

The Son of Night, the Brother of Sleep

1.

It is the wide-awake that saves
us from fantasy, not night
nor half-lit shadows of dusk
or dawn, but a soul yearning

for morning to come, birds
aloft in the soft air of first light,
cars on streets, highways,
people crowding buses

and sidewalks, hurrying to work,
nocturnal dreams set aside,
ignored, forgotten,
distracted by the usual day,

the fascinations of the commonplace.
It is the reasonable tragedy
most suns wake us to,
an ordinary suffering.

Back to me, a boy stands
at a bank's window–blond,
tall, lovely–staring at me
staring, ruining his reflection.

2.

I saw him just that once.
I imagine him dead now
like one of Job's once
blessed sons God failed to revive.

45

It hurts how the dead won't
stay dead, the forgotten
forgotten just because
it's easier to see them at night,

the past more real in dreams.
It is always like that.
You begin to come
back to me. I reach out

to touch you. It rains.
A bird lands on my window
still beating its wings,
frantic to get in. It's winter.

It should have flown south
but forgot to. I cannot
change my dream to save
it. I want you. I want you.

Neaniskos

It is springtime. Gethsemane burns with a green fire.
His followers sleep, two snoring, one wheezing,
the youngest whimpering like a dog as it slumbers.
A gentle breeze chills the air with lingering
hints of an icy winter. The moon is white
and pocked as the bald pate of a Sadducee.
Gnats swarm over a thin pool of water gathered
from dew. After a long night's carousing,
serving feasting legionnaires, wearing no more
than a linen cloth as the centurion who hired
him demanded, a hungry boy picks a fig not yet
ripe or sweet enough to eat. One of twelve
lies prostrate but fully awake as he shifts
himself onto his knees and continues to pray.
Behind him, soldiers march up a hill, some
laughing, some playfully shaking their spears
like children until chastised by their commander.
Only hares and wolves, deserters, slaves, unruly
barbarians need fear their wrath. Yet at the first
signs of their approach an owl hoots, a jackal
yips, frogs croak huskily, lizards scurry
over weeds and twigs, bats flap more loudly
than a flock of birds flying, soaring westward,
tree limbs shake and leaves shudder as winds
surge before a storm, the sound of their feet
pounding on clay and rock awakening the sleepers.
The praying man stands up and oddly smiles.
A Judaean peasant dressed in shawl, tunic,
and sandals kisses him. Another frees his sword.
Tumult. Mayhem. What sense to make of it?
Is it abandonment? Dissolution? Betrayal
upon betrayal? The chaos despair lets loose?
To chase after the others, to save himself,

the boy—'neaniskos,' not precisely 'young man'—
strips off his linen garment—a 'sindon,' whatever
that word might mean, 'tunic,' 'shirt,' probably
not 'loincloth'—as if it were being ripped or torn
off him by a lusting soldier. As wounds shed blood,
Roman torches drip red sparks onto the ground.
Stark naked, the boy flees, runs, runs faster into
the cover of night, the darkness of Jesus and his story,
and disappears, vanishes for good, as if forever.
Who is he? Why did he irrupt into Mark's
gospel only to escape, leave it as a stranger might?
I intend no comparison, analogy, translation,
allegory, or myth.   No similes or metaphors.
No blasphemy either, though I cherish the heresies
lives conspire with to tell their ordinary stories,
those that happen every day, nothing miraculous
about them. It is the enigma of why after
Jay died of a soft sarcoma, Bill from shooting
himself in the stomach, John by poisoning his body
with drugs, Luke from a car crash on 441,
so many friends lost to AIDS, too many to name,
the unseen many of history, why they abide, why
those that vanish from us stay after departure
not as ghosts, but lives unfinished at the end of it all.
I know what I claim in its strangeness makes no sense.
It is the inexplicable deep dark dwelling in things,
in moments, that holiness clings to like a lover
and will not let go. It is the mystery of joy's
sorrows, the ecstasy of the unknown torn from grief.
It is, yes, you, naked, unclothed, the night you
left me, this senseless semblance, the linen garment
you abandoned I hold now burning in my empty hands.

Old Masters

1.

To be a pagan and a Christian without decrying
any contradiction. To study art in the heart's
museum as if love were a gallery of paintings.
Titian could depict the Virgin Mary rising to heaven

on a cloud attended by angelic cupids, uplifted
by the light of the trinity. Or, slightly pouting,
a voluptuous courtesan lying on white sheets
a red blanket spread, a small dog snuggling beside her.

A sly Venus from Urbino. Or an armored, arrogant
Philip of Spain. A bare-breasted, penitential
Magdalene. Marsyas flayed in an horrific scene
witnessed by Titian half-hidden among satyrs.

A pietà. The supper at Emmaus. Actaeon peeping.
Profane. Sacred. Jerusalem. Rome. Or Greece.
The scriptures and Ovid. Plato. Eros and agape.
All Titian made into paintings whatever the passion.

2.

Do you remember one night forty years ago,
after we'd listened to recordings of Glenn Gould
playing Orlando Gibbons and an L.A. consort
under Craft singing Gesualdo while we skimmed

through books of Renaissance Venetian art—Titian,
Tintoretto, Veronese—our legs touching
spread out beneath the coffee table where
they rested, our backs supported by cushions

49

from the couch, how you dog-eared two pages,
each a portrait, The Man with a Glove, The Man
with a Blue Sleeve, and wondered why, why
these two soulful men among many drew us to them.

Next morning, you woke slowly, aroused by a dream.
Two men, two portraits we had looked at. Love-making
seizing what we had seen. And, after, you were still
the man who wore the glove, and I the one in the fancy blue sleeve.

Our Last Christmas

The usual nativity scene: a new born baby,
agèd father, a much younger mother. All blest,
as we are, it is said in church these days, by an absurdity.
Angels. Shepherds. A star. Magi.
Homo factus est,
they say, but in praise of what?   It is first dawn dark and snowing
where we live. Is there anything
more credible than altar candles? For a moment,
you believe again. Mass over, you are startled by a tree,
you tell me, a staunch old oak that should be
dormant leafing icy bright, the scent
of it more fragrant
than spring's in the cold, bare air, blissful as May, time undone
as we are by the suddenness of sunshine on a morning gratuitous
  as this one.

Testament

This is me reading The Tempest
for the last time.
This is a tree, the lone survivor
of a stand,
sap-saddened by solitude, the loss,
the contrast
it knows between then and now,
the desolate land
to which its roots cling like fingers
losing their grip.
No birds nest in its spindly limbs.
No skittish
squirrels climb its peeling bark.
Its bole is infected
with canker, gnarled and pitch black.
No longer do bees
sip its blossoms. No more do
petals rain
on girls and boys below.
The romance
of its boughs, dreamers of the shade
they hid in,
an apple grove's scents in August,
the bed-soft
soil, redolent of fall, of the day
the children
will return to savor its fruit.
This is a tree
that has been hymned by all seasons.
This is Ariel
leaving it. This is at last its last winter
praising it.

IV.

There Is a Peace within Peace that Feels like Sorrow

Say I have a son. I have been told all men long for a son. Say just
after he turns five he starts to fear the dark. To hear his muffled cries,
I keep our door open wide. Three or four times a night, he wakes me
and my wife.   If I read to him, he grows tired and soon quiet. Laid
back down in his bed, he falls asleep quickly.

But a new terror awakens him. I must hold him longer. I must kiss
what frightens him away. I must comfort him more.

Say a doctor insists I not coddle him. Say even my wife begs me to
stop. She can bear it no longer, his cries in the night.

I close my boy's doors. I shut my own so that his tears are useless as
prayers. No night light shines. Yet he stares wide-eyed into the dark.

Say he grows up to be a fine young man. Say he fights through
France's blasted woods like a child dreaming of rats gnawing roots
raw. He's a marksman firing at snipers. An infantryman. A grenade
he throws blows off a kraut's arm.

I have heard on sleepless nights a train brake, its wheels shrieking on
ruined tracks. So my boy shrieks while falling into a crater yawning
yards wide. Bones bark dark. Clothes peeling off flesh like sunburned
skin.

"Nothing" is what my son says to me. "Nothing."

The best lookout by day, I was told in a letter, the sharpest eye at night.

No fighting. No artillery. No enemy moving either way. Just nothing,
nothing to see, my son. Do not worry, my boy, my only child, that I
have turned off your light.

Say in 'forty-six they fly his body home to his wife who lives far away. I
hire a car. Her younger brother drowned in Leyte. She refuses to tell
me the rest of the story. She and her mother live alone. She tidies the
house most days.

For three years it has never quit raining. We stand at the foot of a
makeshift plot. I lean against a wall pocked with stained glass shards
for decoration. A searing heat blows across the crowded yard.

My boy's grave is black as river silt, like soil good for a garden. Say
he sleeps peacefully now, my son, unafraid, behind a door I hated to
close.

Fundamentalism

Working in her garden, Wade's mother wears her manly yard shoes,
rolled up jeans, a checkered shirt, an embroidered vest, cloth gloves
with rubber palms and fingers, and a blue bandana covering her hair
as she prunes her roses. Fifty feet or so behind her, black columns
of hickory, pine, tulip poplar, and oak trunks form a sort of barrier,
their limbs and branches entwined like a jungle thicket.

Wade sits on the stone wall of a bridge. Leaves bristle in the strong
breezes. Another August thunderstorm is on its way. The rhododen-
dron and laurel bushes smell like iron in the metallic air charged far
off by lightning.

At noon, while his father sat in his white oak chair in front of the
choir, his right foot rose and fell in a slow, dazed tapping. His elec-
tric blue jacket hung off his shoulders. Two deacons opened the
rattling church windows. Wind flapped the bible's pages as his father
gaped out at the gathering thunderheads, grackle black and irides-
cent. In their pew, his mother took Wade's hand, as she used to
when he was a boy. "I love it here," she said, whispering in his ear,
gripping his fingers tighter. "And I love Jesus."

In the plot where she is gardening, datura, columbine, salvia, phlox
all grow together in wild profusion. Order does not concern her.
The honeysuckle vines are crusted with nectar, its flowers yellow as
chucked corn. A hummingbird's beating wings are gold, flaking, a
spiderweb tautly threaded through bush twigs deft as a cat's cradle.

Last night, outside the room he had rented for twenty dollars, a truck
sputtered and stalled as with the back of his hand Wade wiped sweat
off a man's brow. No names, no names, he had promised him. His
belly button, shiny and pink, the tufts and patch of hair below, the
upright member, the thighs, the knees, skin the colored of burned
butter, china doll eyes set in a tough guy's head.

In the morning, walking home on a country road after he had left
the motel, he was almost certain he had heard an old time bitty of a
parishioner passing by in a car sitting in the passenger's seat shriek-
ing, "As I live and breathe, it's the preacher's boy, Al," and laugh-
ing heartily on her way to early church. A scruffy stray mutt raced
out of the kudzu across the otherwise quiet road, wagging its tail
as it slowly approached him closer before running faster and fur-
ther away. An eerie orange light, as if from a fire just lit in the hills,
pierced the dawn mist steaming off the asphalt.

His mother waves at him where he sits on the bridge over a creek
almost flooding from a month of daily downpours. A tit mouse lands
on a persimmon branch and, bobbing, cracks a seed. A flicker stares
down at him from a tulip tree. Hazy plumes languidly rise out of a
neighbor's smokehouse's riprap chimney. The world is enough to
believe in. Let it be. Why dream of leaving it?

Ghost of a Boyhood

1. *Purcell's Filling Station*

Me and Preacher are eating vienna sausages and jawing to pass the time at Dwight Purcell's filling station a few months after old man Purcell had disappeared.

The kid working the pumps stops to listen to him every once in a while, but the fat guy under my wreck of a pickup doesn't quit poking at it for a second. It never does sound right to me, not since the day I bought it from my brother. I'm too young to drive it anyway. Don't have a license. But who really cares? Not the sheriff. His youngest boy is a year younger than me and rides a motorcycle zig-zag on the track at school.

Preacher says, Dwight Purcell was so old he was weather-wise in his bones. I've never known a man with such sun-hardened eyes.

Preacher says, His hands were miracles, gnarled from working in too many tobacco fields when young, his fingers all torn-up from thorns, and he still able to work till the day he left us.

The stick he used to help him walk he'd cut from blighted oak that had fallen in his backyard over yonder. He was some strange man, Preacher says. Bent so bad those last years.

Preacher asks me, Do you recollect those giant king snakeskins hanging inside his station? His son's taken them down, of course. Rightly so. Spooked folks.

I say I do.

Dwight Purcell peeled them off the road after a semi had rolled over them, Preacher tells me. That truck flattened them like shiny black crepe paper strips. Beautiful kings, lying smashed on the road in a double S. Dwight figured the two of them twined together like that was a particularly potent sign.

Chewing on a sausage, Preacher looks up at the sky.

Thought clouds spelled out omens, he says. Swore his soldier grandson killed on D-Day had appeared to him in the woods early in '45 to predict when the war would be over. Got it right to the hour almost.

Preacher slurps some more of the salty juice from the can.

Old Dwight. I don't know how he did it. Believed you could see the future in melting snow. In a cat's eye. In the thickness of a man's calluses. Proved it too, sometimes.

Under the shade of a mimosa, wearing a pork pie hat and a denim jacket, Preacher empties the rest of the can of its remaining sausages, chews them fast, unwraps a pimento cheese sandwich, and snaps off the loosened cap of a sweating RC. Though it's July, almost as hot as the hell he warns us about in every fiery sermon, he wears drooping, baggy wool trousers that touch the tops of his spiffy argyll socks. The skin on his hands is pink as plastic and peeling from sunburn.

Preacher's church is Zion Baptist down the road from Dwight's Texaco. You might have heard of it. He's famous in five counties for his lasting conversions. Raised five children on a small tobacco patch and the promise of imminent redemption.

Just seven steps to glory, Preacher likes to say. I was too young to have to have taken more than the two I'd already impressed him with, Preacher reassures me.

Old Dwight Purcell, Preacher says, shaking his head, his pinched eyes shining in the glow of admiration. How he loved his records.

Billie Holiday. Sarah Vaughan.

I used to catch him singing along lying on a mattress someone had tossed behind the station. He possessed the deepest bass voice in our full gospel choir, that's for sure.   Singing along to his records, to the radio inside the station. Made some folks wonder about him. About his faith. Why it wasn't gospel all the time.

I don't expect a man can be perfect here on this earth, Preacher says. Least of all Dwight Purcell.

A man like that, so full of kindness, such a loner. Sad, Preacher says. That old man. I could tell you things about him you wouldn't believe.

I say, I wish you would.

Later, Preacher says. Once we've learned where he slipped off to.

2. *Death*

You'll never find him, Preacher. You weren't there. Only I was.

Only I saw Dwight Purcell taking his canes for a stroll in the woods, hard as it was for him to walk with his bum legs, headed past where he usually walked most nights, far into the pine and oak forest, way beyond where he played as a boy when escaping his chores.

Watch him with me. Already it is dark. His sore, worn out heart is racing. His walk is halt, but steady. Those trees are memory, the clearing he sees ahead, despite his breathing becoming more la-bored, is the light of his past.

A forest will tell you truths no friend would willingly tell you to your face for fear of scaring you to death. Things you'd rather forget or ignore.

An owl perches in a hickory grove that's only half century older than that old man is, an ancient owl watching him watch it preening.

Just as his lungs start to hurt bad, the woods open like a curtain onto the lake. He locates the boat he was told he would find tied to the pier swaying in the wind as if it were about to break in two.

This is what no one understands about that night. Only I can. How he knows where he's going. How he knows where the boat waits. How safe it is. How kind the oarsman is who will row him across. How he already knows the whole story before he leaves his rooms above the filling station.

Tossing aside the sticks he no longer needs, without stumbling or hesitation, he steps into the boat.

Deep in the woods in back of him, hoot owls bid him farewell. Birds of morning salute him goodbye by singing at night.

He sits facing forward, letting his fingers sift through the water, cool to the touch, soothing his pain away. Listening to it lapping against the hull, dripping off the oars, he senses he's drifting like a leaf or twig over the lake, wind-blown, wave-driven to the further shore.

Look how content he is, Death says reassuringly, as he steps out of the boat onto land, eager to meet those greeting him, ready to show him the way ahead, still hard for him to find the right path in the deepest dark.

Look to the woods where I've brought him none living have explored, and I a handsome oarsman, if I say so myself. Look how beautiful he is, Death says. Look at what a pair we make.

3. Preacher Josiah Rowe

I miss him, Preacher repeats as he walks me to his car for a ride to our church. Miss his powerful singing most of all. Never lost that robust voice of his, Dwight Purcell. There's never been a finer bass in our choir.

What really happened to him? I'll tell you, boy. I'm glad you asked. I don't know. No one knows. Don't believe them if they tell you they do.

Abducted by a stranger, robbed of a few bucks maybe, Preacher says. Killed for nothing, perhaps, for the little he had left in his pockets, his body dumped into the lake.

The cops found his canes, all right. But nothing else. No trace of him was ever discovered, not one clue, not even after the sheriff had the lake dragged twice.

He was loved. No one could deny that, no one. Dwight Purcell was loved throughout his life by all God-fearing Christian folk.

A few blame the Klan, Preacher says, Dwight being so softhearted and free-thinking about things like that, about his fellow man and all. But that's nonsense.

Or maybe he got trapped in a cave. Attacked by wild dogs. I've heard every story, all the rumors and gossip. A lot of nonsense. Hooey.

A woman even. Can you believe that, Dwight Purcell, a man sneaking into his eighties and never much of a looker, from what I could see from old photos, taken in, seduced by a woman?

I think he knew death was coming, Preacher says. I think Dwight just skedaddled so as not to cause any inconvenience or bother to anyone. He never did like to be a nuisance.

He was a man for signs, that's for sure. Weather. Sun. Moon. The sky above the tree line where storms begin. Clouds. Lightning. Thunder. Rain.

Everything in life is a sign, boy, Preacher says. Best be advised to pay attention. Old Dwight knew a thing or two better than the rest of us is all I can say,

Preacher swigs the last of another RC and tosses the bottle into a bin.

Time to praise the Lord for His many glories and wonders, kid. I feel the rapture erupting in me.

Choir practice. He opens the door to a battered old black Ford. Jump on in but be careful of those loose springs on the seat nearest the door.

4. Beethoven, Opus 70, #1

I haven't sung in a church choir for over sixty some years. Soon I'll be almost as old as Dwight Purcell was when he disappeared. I lost my faith, what little was left of it after I'd turned twenty, in Vietnam.

After the war, I studied journalism at Chapel Hill, got a job at an anti-war paper in New York, scuttled it after it had failed two times over, picked up work as a reporter at WBAI, stayed there most of my

working life. I've been retired for ten years. I've lived in a studio
in a pre-war rent-controlled building on east 11th for most of many
decades.

I never settled down with anyone. I prefer not to say why. The few
times I've tried I've always been misunderstood. It's what happened to
someone I loved in Nam.

My best friend is Meredith Mims. She knows my story better than
anyone. Over the years away from Carolina, I developed a taste for
music, almost any kind, but my favorite is Beethoven. Despite the
life I've lived in exile, I still feel like a hick at times. I try to hide it.
But I still think of myself that way. Po'bocca, peckerwood, redneck.
I've heard all the names. New Yorkers can be the worst.

Meredith asked me once if I believed in Jesus and his promise of
our salvation. "Almost," I said, because I did and didn't. Belief
gives me hope. It's hard to give up. I used to think I knew what it
meant to believe in something. I don't anymore.

Last night, we went together to a concert by a local piano trio she
had heard was good at Saint Marks. The price was right, it was
close to my apartment, and, despite the onset of winter, the weather
looked fine. We sat toward the back. Sometimes I need to stretch
my legs when they start to twitch without warning at the worst of
times. I try not to make a lot of noise when I have to stand up.

The last piece of three was Beethoven's Opus 70, #1.

Just like me, Meredith was a child of poor farmers, though she has
had more troubling hiding it, from me at least. It's her accent that
gives her away. She escaped northern Alabama quick as she could,
just nineteen. We met when she came to WBAI for an interview.
She'd been arrested for protesting Koch the Monday before. Our
friendship began that long ago.

She's not the fan of classical music I am. If she could still move with any hope of surviving its twitches, she'd be dancing the nights away to heavy metal rock 'n roll.

What was that about? she asked me at a coffee shop we ate at for its coffee and the best pecan or peach pies outside of the South either of us had ever eaten. We both could strand to diet, I guess. Pies and whipped cream are what we thrive on nowadays.

What do you mean by 'about', Meredith? Which one?

The last piece, Wade. The Beethoven. I don't get it.

Oh. I thought you might have meant the Kirchner.

No. I don't care about it. That was just ridiculous. The Beethoven. What was that about?

All right. Let me see. I gazed heavenward. When I was in Vietnam, I began.

She rolled her eyes. Here we go.

When I was in Vietnam my platoon found itself fighting along the Perfume River. There was a village close by. A lot of people were dying there, all over the place, soldiers, civilians, men and women, children killed on purpose or randomly.

Each night, around twilight, as many of the people who lived in that village as could gathered along the banks of the river. They might wait there all night, no matter how dangerous it was.

When the sun rose, they returned to their fields. Strange people. I asked one of the ARVN with us why they kept watch all night long.

He said they were waiting to get to the other side, to the safety they trusted they'd be delivered to on the other side. He said they believed that a wandering soul would come for them in a boat. An ancestor, he said. In the form of a ferryman.

Men, women, and children, afraid for their lives, stretching out their arms in prayer, yearning night after night for deliverance, hoping for a ghost to row them across, to the opposite shore.

You see, Meredith? Do you understand me?

That that is what the Beethoven was about? You can't be serious, Wade.

Yes, I said, I am quite serious. I swear to you. It's about waiting for a ferryman to carry you across. I am certain of it.

And does he come, this ferryman?

In the Beethoven, yes, I said. In the trio's last movement, at least. Not in life. Maybe in death, who knows. But never in life. Not once.

Not ever, I said. Which is why life is far sadder than most music.

Ah, Meredith said. I see. I understand. I thought so. You still believe in ghosts, don't you. Not in God maybe. But in ghosts. You've known too many for one life, Wade.

Have I? I said. Maybe what you say is true. I used to think life was full of ghosts. Yet now I know only music can be haunted. That's ghosts enough, I suppose.

You're disappointed? Meredith said.

Of course, I said. Why shouldn't I be? Why aren't we all? Without ghosts, nothing would be real anymore.

I can't believe that, Meredith said. I won't.

5. Bellevue Hospital

You asked me if I wanted anything. If I needed anything to ease the pain.

I'm not kidding. I would like to be a fifteen year old boy again. As old as I am, who wouldn't, right? I'd like to have the chance to live my life better the second time.   I would try not to botch it as badly again, I promise you.

You see, I think I know where Dwight Purcell went that night when he vanished. I wish I could say the same for my life tonight. About where it is going. I haven't a clue.

Who's Dwight Purcell? Yes, of course. You wouldn't know, would you? How could you possibly know? I'm getting forgetful. How old are you anyway? Twenty five? Thirty?

That young? My.

He was an old man who disappeared when I was just a kid. He ran a filling station. He used to give me a quarter or a dime sometimes. For nothing, just to be kind. Or a free soda. A sweet, generous old man. I thought he was the ancient of days.

He was nearly eighty two or so when he disappeared. Vanished off the face of the earth.

That's the way to die. Not like this. Not shut up in tiny room with no windows.

I'd heard all the stories, but I wanted to find him, at least whatever traces of him I could discover. I thought people might praise me for it if I found a clue or two.

So I explored the shoreline of the lake a half mile or so away from his gas station right after twilight almost every evening for a month, not caring about sleep, ready to swear I went for a late night swim if anyone should catch me out so late.

My father thought I was rutting. That was fine by him. He'd started at the same age, he confided to me early one morning, just as I got home. He winked at me. Who's the girl, Wade?

There was no girl. I was only searching for the boat.

I remember our borrowing it when I was little and my father brought me and my older brother there to fish until it began to leak too bad to use. The pier it was kept tied to had started to rot as well.

The water was starting to get infested with algae, too. This was just a few years after the war had ended. So much had been left to go to hell during those years.

The rowboat was gone for good, nowhere to be found. Finally rotted away and sunk, I guessed. I could spot fragments of the pier where weeds grew around fallen planks or over sunken piles.

One night, though, real late, as I stared across the water, I could have sworn, far in the distance, I saw someone paddling toward me through the mist. I thought it might even be a ghost or some other kind of apparition.

I caught only a glimpse or two of him. Whoever it was, it wasn't Dwight Purcell. It wasn't a grown-up. It was a boy, young as me.

Just some other kid out later than he ought to have been rowing another stolen boat probably.

He stood in the back of the boat, both hands grabbing the oar he used like a pole, propelling it like a skiff.

I don't know why. I got scared. I got to thinking he might be coming for me, to row me over to my doom like he might have old Dwight Purcell.

I hadn't lived most of my life yet. I didn't want to die. I still don't. Bear that in mind.

It was a sight that frightened me so bad I nearly flew home and hid under blankets for the rest of the night in my bed, shaking. I'm still shaking from it. Look. My damned legs.

I never told a soul about it. I didn't want anyone to think me crazy. Until now. Now that I am telling you.

I'm not sure about it anymore. It feels like it all happened centuries before this one. And yet I saw him again just a minute or two after you entered this room. Near as you are working on that bag of blood. Everything filling up suddenly with water, like a lake suddenly rising out of nothing, and he was riding on the surface of it while I stood on the shore, far off, waiting.

I know you're an orderly who's never met me before. Or maybe the night nurse. But I have to tell somebody, don't I? Because I'm sure I can see him. Right now. Right this moment.

Dwight Purcell drowned. I know that for sure now. He drowned himself where no one would find him, no one could drag him up. But someone saved him anyway. Some boy, no matter what he wanted.

Listen. I can hear water lapping. I can hear oars creaking. And a few birds off in woods somewhere singing as if they wanted me to hear them this late at night.

He's coming closer and closer. In all this music I'm hearing, I'm hearing him, I mean. Through the mist, steadily coming, appearing clearer and clearer. Not some ferryman. Not an oarsman. The boy. The first one I fell in love with. Would have rowed to the other side with gladly. Me and him. Long ago.

Ash Wednesday

1.

Ashes from their fires blacken his followers' faces much as his own.
Their eyes wild with disbelief, they stare at him and smile and stifle
tears, bewildered though not inquiring why he is able to be with
them again. As if fresh on his body, his wounds are plain to see,
ember-colored like burns that have not begun to heal.

As he always has done, he enjoys watching his men fish and the
taste of their catch roasted on sticks, sweetly tender. Though cheap
chianti, their wine is pleasant on his tongue. His friends ask him
many questions about death, his and theirs. He offers no answers,
but welcomes the talk of homeless men gathered round a beach fire
made from trash and driftwood.

It is just past dawn on the first day of Lent. Once more, his days
with them are numbered. Saddened, distracted, he gazes at the
rising sun as a madman might do. Is it the earth that is blazing as
on the day he had said he would set it on fire, a vision that burns his
sight without blinding him?

It is a coruscating light none of the others can see as clearly. He
feels himself sweating. It is the death he must suffer again, its pain
like a fever's, this ascendent day, its heartbreaking splendor.

2.

By the ruins of a parapet, an old man stands on the summit of Sutro
Heights. It is a time for penitence, to forgive and be forgiven. The
beach and sidewalks far below are scattered with people returning
after days of heavy rains. The waves are dotted with a few surfers.
By drifting higher and higher, some darkening clouds have managed
to survive the assault of storm-driven winds without breaking apart.

72

The divide between sky and sea is hazy. In every direction he looks,
the world is unhappy. He has lost sight of a flock of sparrows
caught in a gray cloud. The view for miles southward is shrouded in
a lingering mist.

His forehead bears a cross of ash. At bedtime he must wash it off.
Five months ago, exhausted by years of drought, the earth caught
fire. Now weeks of rain flood rivers and valleys.

The cliff on which he stands is a precipice two hundred feet high,
its rock face clutched as if fearful of falling by ferns, algae, lichens,
spiraea. Near the horizon, small as a toy boat, a cargo ship sails
steadily westward as if eager to plunge headlong over the edge of
the world.

Afghanistan

Lea unties the green velvet ribbons that bind her hair, more gray
than brown these days, and lets it fall down freely over her shoul-
ders, gently shaking it, enjoying the feel of it against the back of her
neck. She has not budged from the porch swing all night, rocking,
rocking.

Like words of comfort, the soft dawn is the color of her hands, pale
and slightly ruddy as she rubs them together until it almost hurts.
She wears white lace round her wrists and in the collar of her dress
more lace, fancier, that she knit herself and sewed on where the
cloth was frayed from too much use.

She stares past neighbors' clapboard houses and backyard garages
and over the untamed canebrake toward the river. From a sweater
pocket, she removes the picture of him she had almost forgotten she
still had when she saved it from a small, inherited mahogany chest
she had been compelled to sell, maybe the second best picture she
had of him from overseas, mailed to her from Kabul. He is wear-
ing his helmet and a big grin, not one or the other, but both. What
sense could she make of that?

Peach blossoms fall onto her loosened hair and open lap. She
shakes them off. A stray dog, maybe wild, rustles through brush-
es. She tries to shoo it away, but, failing, treats it with the kibble
her two old hounds are ravenous for. As it laps up the bowl, with
a stove flame she torches the snapshot a fellow soldier, one of his
platoon, must have taken and drops its ashes in the trash can under
the sink.

Ten years have passed almost to the day She has given away her
nights, most of her sunlight hours to the man she has lost. What
was he accused of? He and his men? Taking potshots at children
for the fun of it? No, no. The Lord may be such a monster, but not

her husband. The dog licks her hand, begging for more. She picks
up the bowl. Wide is the road that leads to death. And thousands
walk together there.

She misses them all. She needs a car, a bus, a plane, some means
of escape. It is seven in the morning. Time for a walk. The muddy
shoulder is tangled with weeds and vines. Birds chatter. She wan-
ders across a field and through woods to the river where she sits
cross-legged on a boulder, the water slowly receding from yester-
day's rains.

A sycamore has collapsed during last night's winds, the big blow she
kept watch over. Its trunk is moss covered. Its branches have sunk
into the river. How like a woman's freed long hair they look under-
water, strands of it tossed this way and that in the eddy.

The sun glares through low clouds. Two crows cling to a pine limb
and caw at squirrels shinnying up its trunk. Far off, by a farm, a
hound brays at the last sliver of an April moon. He was a good man.
She knows that. Everyone knows that. Her husband was a good
man. Lea tosses a clay clod into the river to test its strength as it
rushes west through thick brush banked by forest.

Break-up

1.

Reason maddens a man's nature, you said. Winter is who we are.
Or we are summer thunder, the sudden, fierce clapping of blacken-
ing clouds. The seasonal metaphors you used for love whenever you
threatened to leave me.

And your sure departure? Just an end-of-life-season, no cause
for worry or wonder, you said, only the inevitable rot and decay of
springtime declining from its former glory, like desire losing its
longing for a body become too familiar, as curiosity is bored by a
story repeated.

Today, a colorless sun shines on fresh snow. I know what you had
wanted me to see. I was growing too persistent for you to stay.
Like a cold that imprisons you indoors.

The mind chills when it discovers there is nothing left to know, see,
or gain by thinking, the world too bright, the earth so ruined and
shadeless it is dangerous to contemplate.

What you meant to say in another way is that too much thought
might burn a man like ice, freeze the mind, turn it antarctic in its
desolate grandeur. And what could we do anymore, after passion
had died, but think and so mourn?

Without you, I am blank as the reason you derided. White as ash,
maggots, the host I shivered to consume at communion. White as
the turn of every year.

Snow on more snow is how New England survives, you said as you
showed me the frozen pelt of a woodchuck glittering like glass.

Your absence is a meadow blanketed by a blizzard. No grass or field
full of flowers, sun-needy, could shine as blindingly as snow, as my
solitude does.

I miss you. I lock the doors, pull down the shades, close the shutters.
Solitude is safety, the kindness of a December solstice I hide in. I am
a boarder in my own home, despairing of you, my absolute darkness,
the vacuity I've grown used to.

I dreamt of an underground cave last night, a spelunker with a lamp
on the hard hat I'd need to find my way, water drip, drip, dripping
from a bony stalactite. My thoughts of you are like that, limestone
deposits forming on the floor, slowly, slowly taking shape into
something almost human, the mineral soul.

It is hard to breathe in a cave, cold as passionless flesh is, cold as a
desperate mind, its icy terror. Albino fish, translucent, blind, is my
life now. I love you.

I lie awake. Stay away from you. Don't knock at your door.

If you read my letter, may it freeze your heart with its reasonable
madness. With its ardent bitterness. Its numbing passion. May it
bring you back like the dead of winter.

2.

Returning to the estuary, the tide rustles the reeds and cattails
growing out of the moss and boggy ground at the end of a plank
walkway.

There is no moon. The sky is cloudy with stars. Winds blow through
trees fiercer than those we know in the city. Where you walk, thick
weeds crackle.

No TVs, phones, radios, computers. No neighbors. A monkish
solitude by Douglas fir, redwoods, tidal waters receding, flowing
back, steady breezes.

You read novels by daylight, try to meditate when it is dark, eat sand-
wiches, salads, pocket pies from a roadside market in Inverness.

Semis traveling on Sir Francis Drake carrying full milk cans and
crates brake at the curve by our shack, awakening you from bad
dreams while I sleep imagining another morning with you.

Each dawn is like a fire over the hills, burning trees and dry scrub
grasses.

The day you left, fog billowed and spilled and spilled like tide reced-
ing to refill the sea.

More than a century ago, plates clashing, a vast crack forced it
northward. Disasters there's no way back from. The solace that
comes from knowing that fatality.

How catastrophe ruins all understandings, as love does while it is
ending, abandoning me to an island forever divided from the main-
land, and you safe on the other side where you stood your ground,
careless of the danger, of the certain rupture, still within sight until
the temblor subsided.

3.

Pebbles: chipped and flat or round as marbles, all gray as slate, side-
walk cement, the wet fur of a dead tabby, bleached inner tubes, the
cinders left behind when snow
melts on a highway.

Crack one open to discover surprising colors, the rusty ochre of
foam blown by winds and waves across the beach, the pale blues of
a cloudless morning sky, or garnet magenta, raspberry red, sandy
yellow, the egg shell white of the white of an eye.

Or in another pebble, no less smooth, broken apart, to find within it
the gray of its shell a rock concealing nothing or hiding all, the way
ghosts stay wisely unseen in the night they abide by.

Suppose a Buddha carved from smoky colored stone, massive as if
sculpted from a cliff, a Buddha like the one in the Asian museum
whose eyes are closed as he gazes at a bay where sea-starved sailors
mount the walkway into a docked ship painted on a wide silk screen,

suppose that that mammoth statue crumbles one day into pebbles
like these lying shoreside waiting for waves to tug them back to sea
while mist like minuscule clouds evaporates from them, from the
sand they lie half buried in or into which they appear to have dug,
to escape a fiery sun as coquina or crabs do,

pebbles, friable stones:

as if matter could be by matter dissatisfied, broken into small gray
pebbles cast in, dragged out by hazard of waves, polished, washed
clean, dark as driftwood, some all gray, some bright and various
as petals inside, their colors, plain gray or daring, repeating the
prayers rocks chant after their shattering has revealed within them:

mineral omens of a passion

that I claim for truth.

Mourning Patrick

His three bedroom windows looked out on a cramped midtown
Manhattan: four plain tenements, a couple of old low rise brick
businesses, three billboards, a half dozen traffic signs, a lonely,
spindly tree on the southeast corner. It had no real view to speak
of, straight down only sidewalk, parked cars, and taxis winding in
and out of lanes.

Yet it was that vantage, near the end, apart from us, it was that
stark reminder of its failures, as he saw them, that bore witness to
his life. It lacked vision or revelation. It was ordinary.

At least once a week, while he was still well enough, he took pains to
arrange fresh bouquets of the tulips, roses, irises friends bought for
him at a neighborhood shop. He cut the stems and carefully placed
each flower into porcelain vases.

Sometimes a glimmering light shone into this room off the snow
that had fallen overnight onto nearby roofs. Once or twice, sun rays
refracted by a crystal goblet he displayed on a windowsill cast a
rainbow pattern on a plump pillow or folded sheet.

There was in his apartment nothing in bad taste, nothing grandiose,
Pat would say. No intimations of greater things. Just small, modest
objects in their lesser way aesthetically sufficient. Lovely common
flowers. Prismatic colors shining suddenly on his bed. Framed
photos of family and friends. A Paul Klee poster.

On the glass of each sketch or drawing, on the base of each objet, he
had pasted a tiny sticker with the name of the person he meant it to
be given to once he was gone.

Orderly is how he would have it. He knew the days of his dying
couldn't be peaceful. So he chose to be orderly after his death in-
stead.

Sitting beside him, a young priest he barely knew whom the church
had sent over placed his hand upon his withered left arm without
having to be asked. Like some happy chance of a trick whom he
might have picked up in bar years ago, he did what Pat longed for
him to do without his having to be asked. It was not, in this in-
stance, that he touched him without compunction. It was that he
was kind. He was gentle.

Pat's beard had not been shaved in days. So Father Mark shaved
him.   It was like watching a sculptor carve away clay from a face as
an old handsomeness returned.

His friends waited in his living room, our eyes gazing helplessly on
small vases, tiny sculptures, a few icons, a crucifix, a mateless can-
dlestick that Pat, laughingly, claimed to be a self-portrait, a solitary
thing of tarnished pewter and dripped wax. In the kitchen down the
hallway, a woman none of us seemed to know prepared our chicken
soup and salad lunch.

Near the end, he could not talk anymore or rather when he did at-
tempt to speak his words were hard to understand. He quit trying
to communicate, ate little, spent all his days and nights awaiting the
end in his rented hospital bed, greeting each dear friend in turn with
the same uncomprehending gaze with which he would stare down at
the street, perplexed by who it might be he watches trudging alone
in the snow, why is he there, why is anyone here or there, the vex-
ing question of whether it was immortality or oblivion he was facing
whenever he looked out a window, the mockery it seemed to make of
things, the futility of it all.

If asked, I would tell you this first about Patrick Cummings. He was
a faithful friend to us all, a good son to his parents, a good brother to

his two sisters, an ardent lover to a few, too few he'd say, me among
them, and honest, always honest even when he did not mean to be.
Close to the end, he confessed to me that he had never known the
life he had hoped for.

I think he meant, among other things, he had hoped for a life of
prayer.

The moon was a burnt orange the Maundy Thursday night Patrick
died, far larger than a mere full moon, a late winter haze in the air,
desolate as smog, that neither the snow nor rain had managed to
clear, a haze that ballooned the moon beyond all due recognition. A
monstrous, marvelous full moon.

The scene on Golgotha would begin again at noon the next day, Fa-
ther Mark reminded us. Father Mark often dwelled on the passion
of our Lord.

Thirteen men, Father Mark said, none a betrayer. All share in the
meal. Remember me, Jesus beseeches.

Remember him.

I see his hair, his moonlit eyes, his chest, thigh, knees, his hands ex-
ploring what more there was to know about my face.

Memory is venereal, the nakedness, the passion it recalls more last-
ing than the nakedness that inspires it.

The evening Pat and I went on our first date, at his bidding, we took
the subway up to the Heights where we strolled the grounds of The
Cloisters watching a half moon slip into a fog bank that was drifting

deeper into the harbor. A cold wind blew a frosty spume onto our faces. We held hands.

I would say, at least today, that on the night he died the moon in its glory stopped shining on us, that it would no longer bother to spy through the windows into the room where we had lived together, that it chose to quit illuminating the passion to which it once had borne witness, no shades drawn, no curtains closed, our unashamed nakedness, plain for all to see. Naked before God, Patrick would proclaim.

The nakedness Pat admired most in any painting when it showed what was revealed when the body was stripped down to its spirit.

The nakedness, he would say with a blasphemer's sly grin, of Jesus on the cross.

The memory of whatever is most real about us.

Pat told me many stories the first weeks we were together. I will set down only two.

1.

Fifteen, no seaman, he was taken on a fishing trip off Long Island by an elderly friend of his mother's who, even as the boat encoun- tered a squall causing men to slip on the wet deck, the boat to rock, a few to vomit over the railing, calmly ate the tuna sandwiches and pickles he had brought for lunch.

Pat had refused both, of course, fast removing himself to the cabin to wait the storm out in safety, the men huddled in it hunched over, afraid, saying nothing, not wanting to show they were scared as the boat rolled in high waves.

Pat wiped his breath off one porthole to make it clearer, wanting to
see past the lashing storm, the leaning, lurching stern to where the
sea might be claiming the boat and them all soon.

Half in a daze, he was wondering if this was the most of fear he
would ever need to know until intrepid Fred pointed to a school
of flying fish leaping and playing in the sea, at home in the storm.
Wonderful, Fred Garrett said and chomped on a pickle.

2.

Twenty years after, in the Olympics, on the Hoh River Trail, waking
at dawn, having walked far enough away from camp to take a pee,
Pat saw, in the pale light, a bull elk and its herd racing back and
forth in the rainforest, almost in circles.

He hid behind a giant spruce, but the bull spotted him and stopped
suddenly in its tracks, looking ahead and behind itself like a lost
hiker. Something about Pat attracted it slowly toward him, not
preparing to charge, just curious, Pat guessed.

He stepped out from where he had been trying to spy upon the
herd unseen and lay down in the moss, giving himself to something
greater, more important than he was, to the bull elk, the cows, the
air so drunk with light, thick with dew, he thought he might drown
in it, lying there, nothing happening, no returning to life until they
trampled him or left.

Pat referred to them as stories he liked to relate from his own life
about moments he'd experienced of grace. I would like to say I
agreed with him.

I return too often in my old age to the final scene. Windows shut,
shades drawn, draperies closed, a bedroom lit by candles flickering
in the stilled morning air. Pat's body white as the freshly ironed

84

sheets that failed to cover him. From an incense burner, the smell
of rosewood perfuming the calm of dawn.

A prayer would be good now, the young priest said.

Your room felt like a room a boy had lived in when young and aban-
doned. Like old men's bodies can sometimes look.

Forgive me. As I looked away from where you lay, I thought of the
two of us making love, thrashing about, rolling to the bed's edge,
grasping, embracing, kissing, not knowing at any moment exactly
who would do what to whom until getting tired we stopped for a
while, but only for a while, taking deep breaths before resuming our
love making. What were we searching for, trying to reach? Ecsta-
sy, you insisted.

Ecstasy. Passion. Forgive me. I was thinking about why it quit
happening. Our joy. The folly in our believing it would last.

Why shouldn't love making be a knowledge of God? you'd ask. But
why must it be, Pat? Why that or nothing?

Out of nowhere one night as we prepared for sleep you announced
to me you would be leaving for Paris the next day. Would be gone
for months. I should not have been shocked, I suppose. It was our
usual rift, the constant teetering on a break-up, the question of
whether we wanted more for the rest of our lives, whether together
or alone.

The week you returned, we hiked upstate through the loveliest
meadows in the world, you maintained, to a lake few knew about
northwest of Syracuse, quiet, windless, peaceful, ducks floating
like decoys in the shadow of an afternoon sun, no birds singing, no
leaves rustling in an uncanny silence.

I guess it was a place you took me to for us to confess about the tricks or boyfriends we each had had while you were away in France.

Some secrets exposed are unsurmountable. Woods, rocks, a knob of a mountain, its slopes, the sun, the play of new light in a radiant sky. The mystery of beauty remains of course. But not our lives, not once a love has been revealed to be so meaningless, so reckless in its faith as to tear the world apart.

Rest your arm on mine, Pat. Let us wake one more time to the morning sun gleaming through the windows, the sheets we lay on wet with dew.

It is enough now. It must be enough. To mourn must be more than enough to believe in the love within it.

Plato was wrong about many things, but none more than this. What we discover in the cave we live in all our lives, in the darkness we cannot escape from, what we see by the flames we throw on its walls is what is most true. I mean the shadows a life casts from the fire inside it upon a cave wall is more real than anything it would learn outside it, less dark and mysterious.

It's another overcast sky this morning, dingy, mud gray. A north wind blows frigid air through Manhattan, stark, rheumy, threatening a late snow. Uptown, the few people out obediently waiting for the light to change before they cross huddle together on curbs against the cold. I'm wearing a scarf pulled tight around my neck, the leather bomber coat you thought was hot I am too old for, fleece lined gloves, shit-kicker boots. I must look a fool.

Block after block, my soles click on the icy sidewalks. Two sub-
way rides and I am there where your ghost has summoned me, The
Cloisters miraculously open on so cold a morning.

I go straight for your favorite image, the plaque of the Pentecost
painted in holy blacks, vermilions, viridians, cobalt blues against
a field of gold. You are to me, Pat, the figure on the far right, one
of the truly assembled. It is you I pray to. I knew it all along, how
special you were, your face, the brightness of you, radiant with the
Holy Spirit.

Snow cloaks the roofs, fire escapes, ledges of the buildings across
the street where I live now, like you at the end alone. Aerials, poles,
slack wires forest the tenements. Black clouds drift over head. The
February sky is hushed and sunless. Our bodies are like a book.
In memory, they fold together as seamlessly as paper sheets along
the crease. So I offer you to read me, turning pages of our shared
memories.

Neither of us can return to sleep after late night sex. In the morn-
ing, we hike to Battery Park to watch the ferries dock and commut-
ers disembark, pigeons, swarming among their feet, paying little at-
tention to the human commotion around them. Workers are fitting
girders on the top of a new building.

We drink coffee, eat strudel sitting on stools in a small cafe, stroll
silently uptown. As we pass by store windows, like a film frame
melting on a screen, our bodies blur on sunlit glass.

Near the park, the wind rattles the tree limbs along its stone walls.
The tang of horse flesh and piss lingers in the air after a hansom cab
nears us and drives past, its giddy passengers waving back at us.

Such happiness as we know.

I touch your sable hair, Pat. I smell your skin. I taste your tongue tasting mine. I miss you, the joy you gave me on the last day as on the first, the unending beginning of the incarnate world, you assured me to console me, knowing I would not believe you until it was too late for us both.

Manhattan in the Forties

An uptown Victorian: maroon upholstery, umber woodwork, vast
rose-rust velvet curtains to shield eyes from too much light, indoors
or out. The musty smell of rooms whose doors are always closed.
Brown out, war on, gas lamps low. Smoke clings to glass and plas-
ter like fungus. No matter how hard she wipes, the maid cannot
sweep away the dust that seeps through walls and thin glass panes.
For which disgrace, the elderly lady of the house will not apolo-
gize. Porcelain black, a cat arches its back on a bookcase, leaps,
creeps across a Persian rug to claw, gold-surprised, on a string of its
threadbare unraveling pattern.

Friday, after he quits hauling trash off the streets of the lower east
side, Colin orders a beer at a neighborhood bar where the barkeep
offers him weekly tips on the ponies running the harness races at
Vernon Downs upstate. Following his gut, he places a second bet
on the Dodgers, winners, losers, what a life. For a third chance to
feel lucky for once, he plays the numbers, using as his guide the
total of the sins Father had calculated he'd committed last week
at confession early that morning. He swills a frothy while two-bit
mobsters wait for him to pay up or else in the poolroom in the back
of the Shamrock Bar.

Clutching her shawl in her cramped rented room in Hell's Kitchen,
clawing at a letter from her grandson Vincent just released from
SingSing, Anna Nini believes God must be like gravity and she a wave
falling and rising between earth and moon until she breaks upon
the shore. "No more Anna Nini," she says to the stain on her wall,
tap-tapping her World's Fair spoon against an empty coffee cup.

Maybe her father did forbid her to marry him, his skin suspicious-
ly dark. Maybe that shot from his pistol meant to miss his mark.
Maybe her brother's hatred for them both is a hell nothing can save

her from. What's done is done. God knows she is no saint. But in
the midst of a war bloodier still can anything this bloody turn out
well? She rips apart another column from the scandal sheet and
takes a swig that empties the bottle. Who says she wasn't almost a
star back when? The bulb and cord dangling above her swing this
way and that like there's a drunkard loose in the room, a bounder as
free as the streets of Greenwich Village.

Nights are a tunnel, an underground cave, a hole to hide in. Scur-
rying rats, crying bats. The buzz of bugs on the screen. Leaves
rustling against his window from the only tree on his Fulton Street
block. If lights went on across the street in Deana's room, he'd
stand on a chair to see the blonde hairs on her arms, glistening as
she lays her clothes out for morning.

At the Met, Cio-cio-san stands in the middle of the Bridge of Regret
that curves over the River of Sighs. Behind her lies her girlhood,
canebrake, and rushes through which she has just passed on her
way to the stage, her movements lovely as calligraphy. A white her-
on glides on the backdrop, its flight the stroke of an artist's brush.
Her womanhood waits for her high on a hill, the tea house and the
House of Pleasure far below. She passes an old man on the path she
has chosen, a cricket cage dangling from a pole resting on his shoul-
der. Butterfly is already singing her entrance aria while on the crest
above her her American soldier waits for his fifteen year old bride
and, in the last row of the balcony, James rests his hand cautiously
on Cameron's knee.

The No Vacancy sign that shines outside his window bleeds through
the shut blinds. On the unlocked door, on thin useless walls, bright
lines hard as prison bars blink on and off to the tick tock of a cheap
clock he keeps near a night stand. How fast it runs. He closes his
eyes. Useless to try to escape, useless to flee, the long night done
with him before he was born. The stairs outside his room creak

with the pounding of many men's feet. You're still wet behind your ears, still a kid, his brother had said. Naive. He can hear the horn of the Staten Island ferry preparing to sail. The big boss never lies. In the seedy bar downstairs, guys he thought were his friends drink their whiskey straight without having to pay and plug the jukebox full of nickels just to pass the time.

Dressed in black, her page boy haircut fuller than most, she raps her fingernails against the lion's paw arm of her chair. "No," she says. "No. No. No." Her nostrils flare as the others point to the glass. She wants to die. She has always wanted to die, but will not if she is ordered to. Their fear offends her. She has hung a noose in her room since despair makes her more hopeful. No one will see her kick the chair from under her feet. It will be graceful, really, death working the rope-strings of her puppet body like a dancer's, the fall less a drop than a leap, plié.

Time Square lures him like a pulp book cover. A barker wearing a weather-worn, snap-brim fedora tugs on the sleeves of two marines. Globes hang in a triad in front of a honky tonk bar where soldiers on leave sing, "Who Wouldn't Love You." Across the street, a G.I. fires rifles at metal targets in a shooting gallery. Two hookers wearing short yellow skirts stroll past, their arms linked, their heels clicking on the sidewalk. The hot night sweats. He stops where the sidewalk and street are slashed by slats of light from a window to read a sign, Cheap Rates By Day By Week. An ancient Chinese woman in slip-slop slippers passes a young woman wearing a blue cotton frock and Minnie Mouse white high heels. He sniffs grease, smoke, malt sticking to the humid air. The bars are packed as troop trains.

Blackout, shades drawn, curtains pulled closed no more. Standing high above the others startled out of their slumber by a frightened doorman, Catherine wakes to find herself walking on air. The church clock strikes seven. A policeman blows his whistle. Though she can smell bread baking and coffee brewing, breakfast almost

ready, she lifts her skirt and climbs a cloud as easily as stairs. Her
mother snaps, "How dare you." Her father orders, "Come down."
Her brother cries, "Catherine, I believe in you." Too happy to reply,
she smiles at heaven. Her loosened hair streams bright as dawn.
Or bright as moonlight on the bridge she dreams of that she and her
sweetheart are crossing, each gliding step upward like two dancers',
he holding her tightly as she gently executes her point work, the two
of them together, like Fred Astaire and Ginger Rogers in The Bar-
cleys of Broadway, dancing the night away, stars shining bright as
footlights on the stage where a small boy first saw to his delight the
wonders of New York.

Massachusetts

Each spring, the river near my home floods and soaks the earth, bringing soil from upstream, retrieving and spreading sediment wherever it overflows its banks. In summer and autumn, rain falls; in winter, snow. I tell you it is true that dreams need to be refilled, replenished, so much they spill. Let me return to my first world, its storms and turbulent waters.

I am a man asleep, drifting in the middle of a lake as a squall forms over head. I've let the oars I was using to row my boat float off. My coat's torn. I shiver in the cold. I am poor man. The river surges before emptying into the lake, a sight as beautiful as excess can sometimes be. Think longing. Think florid meadows. I am a man like you, drifting in a rowboat in the middle of a lake.

The sassafras in Massachusetts smells good. Hard rains are relieving the trees of their leaves. Golds, scarlets, rusts. A man's days are like grass, the bible tells us. I would add to what the good book says like bent weeds, too, broken reeds, beetle-infested evergreens, or the shed colors of New England forests.

I am a boy in woods, in a cave, in a rain stained house by a bridge over a creek. What has pained me most down through the years? My mother weeping by our well. A red rust wound in a dead dog's hide. My father who shot him.

I am floating on a lake in the middle of a storm. I've let my oars drift off before. Small waves slap against the sides of my rowboat. If I grieve for myself, I grieve for all.

I was in love once, briefly, long ago. His hair glittered with sawdust on a fair, hot, breezy day, the sun glaring in his eyes. Soot from a muffler he was working on smudged his cheeks. A hole in his coveralls, a rip in his drawers, lice I picked out from his soft pale hair, his fingernails gritty and gray from dirt. His smile flared at me like

a quick spreading fire. I remember the shiny buttons on the boldly
patterned shirt he claimed he had stolen from my brother.

The sky forms ribbons of blue, stone gray, ebony. Who drowns in
one life rises in another. So I believe. So memory proves. I hear
my last life slapping against rocks like waves' lapping at the end of
their journey along the shoreline.

Water is what I must mean when I say I desire you still. A lake is
made from the same stuff as the sky. Look how clouds drift on either
like breath across a mirror.

I am a man in a rowboat floating without guidance. Overgrown
bushes clutter the banks leaving scant space for shorebirds to rest
on. Sleep is where thunder rumbles, winds howl loudest, piercing
through the spindrift. I am an old man soaked to the bone, drifting
freely.

Like an enraged parent beating his errant child, a big blow shakes
the trees on shore, toppling one that cracks as it falls. Limbs and
trunks sink deep into the lake's bottom, settling into the mud and
silt and slime of a sunken childhood, the boy who drowned there,
letting go of it all.

A family, not mine, comes to save me. They are packing their
tents and belongings, preparing to leave when a low moon reveals
to the older son a rowboat adrift with no one in it. They form a
search party, scour the shore with flashlights. But night is quick-
ening and they must depart for home before it grows much darker,
the family I would have asked to let me join them in a better life.
The compassionate family of nocturnal wanderings I thought I
should tell you about.

There's a lake near Lee in New England I think of often. I've written of it here. I am the man in the rowboat. I am all he has not done with his life, his longings are my own. I'm no one. I'm anyone. An outcast. I'm a farm boy, a drifter, a lonely man who knows nothing more than what he's dreamed of, floating on a lake in western Massachusetts.

1.

During the year before she marries his father, his mother rides the Hudson ferry daily from Hoboken to work in Manhattan.

When the weather is fair enough, she grips the rails while she stares at the white water expanding behind the boat, the waves traveling in a bobbing V, like geese beating wings against a gray sky,

against desolation as she watches all things flowing beyond her reach.

2.

On the afternoon of his father's thirty-sixth birthday, he and his wife are listening to the Saturday matinee broadcast of Die Walküre from the Met. She's knitting, he's flipping through Time magazines. Her son waits curled in his mother's womb.

Her eyes are happier, her face more radiant than her son will ever be able to know as she sits across from his father busying her imagination by making patterns out of yarn. His father puts down his magazine to attend as intently as she to Wagner on the radio, Wotan's Farewell and the Magic Fire music playing through their speakers on a cold rainy day in northern Jersey.

Far, far away, soldiers are fighting in snow on the outskirts of Moscow, Jews are being shot in Lvov, Japanese planes are flying toward Pearl.

3.

The yard of her son's boyhood is a grove of redbud, dogwood, deodar cedar, magnolia, loblollies, oak. In winter, her husband daily fills his bird feeders with suet and seeds. In spring, it is a kind of paradise, azaleas, January jasmine, camellias, gardenias, forsythia, roses.

In summer, a Carolina sun plays on the leaves, tall weeds, pine needles as on their swimming pool seen from underwater.

Eyes open while he swims holding his breath, her son sees the world brighten above him, darken below, the sun shimmering on the surface as catfish or minnows or trout in a pond might view it, intensified, refracted by passing through water, the distorted light of their universe.

His mother watches him dripping poolside, toweling himself dry. A bee buzzes on a screen. A cardinal drinks from a birdbath. She sits by a window, sewing a button on his shirt for church tomorrow.

4.

Not the stomach cancer but the operation for it kills her mother. In her grief, for the only time in her life, she confides in her son, telling him her last night's dream.

She's standing on the Weehawken Palisades. Suddenly, gazing down into the Hudson, she lets herself go, lets herself fall into its currents, drift past Manhattan, the ferries, barges, liners, tugs, not swimming but floating all the way out of the busy harbor into the vast Atlantic.

She smiles at him. It's funny, she says. I think I spotted your father hoeing a row of beans on that Staten Island farm his family once owned. He waved at me as I passed by.

Why? her son asks her. Why did you jump in your dream, Mother?

Oh, I don't know. Who knows why you dream anything? She

97

shakes her head. I have no idea.

She sighs a little and takes another sip from her mother's prized mug.

She used to delight in watching boats sail out of port from her roof, she says. And there was that affair with a Norwegian sea captain that failed, of course, the romance my father had agreed to since he was almost forty years older than she and had been ill for so long, bedridden for years.

I've told you about that, haven't I? About what her loyalty to my father cost her?

She sips her coffee, blows on it to cool it some. For a moment, her upper lip is stained by froth.

She was always so strong, my mother, proud of her shiny auburn hair, not a gray strand anywhere to be found, not a wave in it she was not born with she bragged until the day she died, if to no one more attentive at the end than me. You know something funny? I envy her vanity.

She smiles at her son again, more soberly, as the desolate some-times smile to be spared more tears.

My mother liked to dress every day in tight fitting silk dresses, blue or red or a few all in black. At parties, more than a bit of flirt, I suppose it is fair to say, she'd dare men to test her firm stomach with a punch. She never wore a girdle, my mother, never. She never had to. No one ever tried to hit her, of course, not in my pres-ence anyway.

Your grandmother enjoyed embarrassing me sometimes. Too often maybe.

She sets her mug on the kitchen counter and gazes out the window
at the rain.

We're having another morning when it pours without stopping, she
says breaking her momentary lapse into silence, one torrent after
the other for weeks it seems.

You know she was born in Holstebro, of course, his mother says. I
believe it is where she would have wanted to be buried after she
died if she had been given a choice, back in Denmark, I mean. She
did miss it.

Floating all the way home, traveling on the Gulf Stream among
some swarming schools of fish. She laughs lightly, almost merrily.
That's how I dreamed of her. Floating across the Atlantic to the
North Sea.

Her voice grows so much softer as she talks he is uncertain if he
should ask her to speak more loudly.

She loved to swim as much as I do. I wanted to join her, I suppose.
So I jumped, his mother whispers to him.   I just plunged in.

She looks at him as a teacher might who wonders if he has been dis-
tracted from listening to her in class by another student.

Don't, her young son pleads with her. Please don't.

Oh, it was only a dream, Silly, his mother says, straightening his
hair where it has flopped over his forehead.

5.

Storms have reduced the sloping, wide, white beach to a plank-nar-
row strip of sand, broken shells, and craggy black boulders. The
seaweed on the beach lies tangled in piles like kindling prepared for

a nighttime fire. Their cottage's stilts appear to have waded into the Atlantic. Slat fences gird eroded dunes.

It is his parents' anniversary. His mother kicks off her shoes, throws her kerchief and straw hat to the wind, lets it sting her face and twist her hair into knots.

She is a girl again, running through sea oats and over the sand. How she would like to dig for crabs with a toy shovel again or build a castle with moats and a wall, she tells her son before she dives into the water.

But the sea and sky are turning thundercloud gray, scaring the sand-pipers, plovers, and gulls away from the beach. As proof of her brav-ery, perhaps, she begins to swim too far out. As the waves surge ever higher, her family calls her back.

A riptide is dragging her further from rescue. She cries to her son, shouts to her boy. Harsh winds batter oats and whip wave crests into funnel spouts that skitter across the sea. A fence that twists around one dune snaps as a breaker crashes over a pier.

Her son swims as fast as he can, fighting the tide to reach her. She clings to him, terrified, unable to move. In her fear, she struggles against him.

Slowly, he coaxes her back to shore where he lifts her onto the warm sand so she can walk, with support, by her own strength. But her husband, her daughter and he must help her up the deck's stairs.

Her breath eases some, is less desperate as she sips some tea from her own mother's antique mug, the one she brings with her wherev-er she goes, the double-size cup with Jeg elsker dig printed on it in blue below a scene of dikes and a windmill.

After her ordeal, she tries to sleep on a couch in the cottage. Something in her posture, in how she rests curled into herself, recalls a sea-creature he had seen a day or two before.

Having been hooked or netted by fishermen who had abandoned it on shore for nature to do with it as it would, it was half dead, its scales shining in the sun, its back slivery, its fins opalescent. Its gills pulsated, a living thing trying to breathe the air of a foreign world it could not survive in.

6.

She lies on her bed in a hospital room. Her son's aging fingers softly skim her white body, touch her face, lips, gritted teeth.

Now swim, Mother, he would say to her. Try.

But death is tugging her further below the surface than an ocean could. He would close her eyes to stop their staring at him, to hide their despair. He should call a nurse.

The room is underwater dark. They are dreaming a dream together, he and his dying mother.

Holding her as tightly as he can, he kicks upward, toward air, toward light, whatever he needs to do to save her from drowning, lifting her, carrying her back to the life, the everyday life despite her loneliness, her fears of it, she had loved.

But she who had always been a daring, bold swimmer was too exhausted to struggle against the tide any longer,

she, who might have dragged him down with her deeper into her dreams, beyond returning,

she freed his arms that were trying to hold her on to her still, let him go.

In his bedroom, he has just hung the last picture she managed to paint before Parkinson's made her hands tremble and shake.

It depicts an early spring dawn in Central Park after a heavy rain, before another deluge hits the city. All is wet.

In her water color of the scene, a granite gray boulder melts like snow. Three narrow, ink-dark, rubber-limber trees bend and twist, two of them crisscrossing as if they were dancing. Like the grass, all the leaves shine an April shower pale green.

In the heavy mist her brush has washed over everything, the park's scrub bushes weave their thin limbs into veils frail as lace. On the West Side, skyscrapers loom like storm clouds billowing. Icy white, blue-flecked, the sky is drenching the world.

It is as if she sees too late, as her sight dims, as she closes her eyes for the last time, the great city fading, the whole wide world dissolving right before daylight broke for good.

Anubis

1. 1945

Roy Sutton is four when the war ends. Of the years before, he re-
calls little more than his mother's making jelly from their backyard
grapes by candlelight, taller, thicker candles in the den where they
huddled for safety behind its boarded windows, he, his brother, and
his mother praying for the hurricane to pass without harming them
or their town, and the cartoon his mother showed upside down from
a small rented projector on a sheet tacked to a wall while he and his
friends, gathered for his birthday, stood on their hands or lay on their
backs on the floor to watch it, giggling and laughing, his mother be-
coming more flustered each time she tried to fix it and right the image.

He was born after his father had been drafted and sent overseas.
He doesn't remember missing him. If he did, his dog Luke would
comfort him, a collie his mother let sleep with him in his bed to
console him, he guessed, though she never said so. Can a boy miss
someone he has never met?

He didn't need stuffed bears or pandas or even a lion to hold. He
had Luke to keep him warm at night, Luke to play with during the
day, Luke to follow him around through the house and outside into
the park next door or the woods behind his mother's garden. He
had Luke to watch over him, to bark when he should be fearful, to
warn him of any danger ahead.

Most mornings, his mother would stand by a window in the living
room, tugging back the curtain as her left hand gripped a handker-
chief while she stared out. She barely noticed what he and his older
brother were up to. She didn't care while she kept watch. Not that
either of them was ever wild or a truly bad boy. But she seemed
not to see them, to know they were there.

Sometimes they fought. Sometimes they broke an ashtray or a glass or yelled too loud or cried after bumping an elbow or pinching a finger. Sometimes they left cars from their train set or pieces from a puzzle or scattered bits of coloring paper all over the floor or even on the stairs to their bedrooms. Many afternoons, their mother would retreat to hers for a while. After her nap, she would ask them kindly to be better boys. But what had they done so wrong?

The day she received the letter informing her her husband, Captain Frederick Sutton, would not be coming home after all, she tried to hold her sons so tightly to her bosom that they both pulled away. It was late summer. The house was warm. That night, either she or his brother, distracted by their grieving, forgot to shut the backyard gate and lock it.

When he woke up the next morning, Roy did not at first remember when Luke crept out of his room, nudged the screen door open, and left, abandoning the family that loved him. It was all a blur.

He knows Luke didn't mean to leave them. Roy is sure of that. Nor did his father. Both meant to come back. But they got lost.

The gate had always been kept carefully locked every time anyone opened and closed it behind them. His mother was scrupulous. He had thought of escaping, too, more than once, of exploring the woods alone, hiking deeper in than he was allowed to go. But how unhappy his mother would be if he did.

For weeks or maybe even months Roy couldn't say 'Luke'. Each morning, after waking, he would throw off his sheets and look out

the window, hoping his dog had been able to sniff or trace his tracks

back, had found his way home. But he couldn't say 'Luke.' And he
couldn't say 'father' or 'daddy' or any word like it. His mother for-
bade him. Denied him because of the pain of it, she said.

2. 1952-3

Roy is eleven when his mother, driving too fast up the driveway,
runs over Fella. He and his brother wrap their dog, more Jon's than
Roy's really, in an old blanket and bury him in the woods close to
their fence.

Not knowing what to say, his mother says nothing. She teaches fifth
grade and is usually quiet at night, grading tests, reading papers,
preparing her classes, watching a little TV with or without her sons.
It is a silent house in many ways. Few words well spoken, his mother
would say.

A year later, she brings home for her boys a puppy from the pound.
Four years older than Roy, his brother is not interested in another
pet, especially now that he has a girlfriend who lives in the neigh-
borhood. Roy names the dog, a cocker mixed with who knows what
other breeds, Blackie.

Blackie is not spayed. His mother thinks it inhumane to spay a dog.
To rob it that way.

When Blackie is fully grown, he begins to howl by day and night,
though more loudly and persistently when it's dark. Roy cannot
sleep with him in his room. He loves him. But none of them can
sleep except when Blackie is locked into a spot in the basement where
a bed has been made for him with a blanket folded in a basket. But
he howls even more when trapped there. His cry is muffled, but they
can still hear him.

He digs in the grass of the yard, digs holes in his mother's garden, uproots flowers and tomato plants. And he often burrows under the fence to escape.

"He's horny," his brother tells Roy. "He's after a bitch. He can smell one from miles away, I bet, when they're in heat."

Roy is only beginning to understand what such words mean, 'bitch' and 'heat' and 'horny'. He has observed Blackie humping pillows, cushions, even his own arm once, watched the seed gush out of him almost identical to his.

Roy has begged him, pleaded with him, but he wails all night and much of each day anyway. The dog doesn't seem to understand the danger, the risk he's taking by trying Roy's mother's patience.

"He hates being left alone. He needs a steady girl," Jon says.

If he is gone, has escaped, when he comes home from school, Roy will ride his bike to hunt for him, calling out his name over and over. When he finally finds him, he links his leash to his collar and walks him back home, guiding his bike with his other hand.

The search sometimes takes him hours riding throughout his neighborhood and other parts of town, running, frantically explor-ing the park and even into the woods. He is afraid he might lose him for good.

He is getting behind in his studies. He worries about Blackie all the time. All the time, he says to his mother. She does not appear to hear him until one morning she says, "I cannot bear it anymore, I can't, Roy." Blackie is lying under the breakfast table, hoping for a treat or a bit of egg snuck to him, wagging his tail.

The next day, as he's rough housing with Blackie in the den, he sees through a window a station wagon drive up and park at their walkway. A large family spills out. His mother grabs Blackie's leash from its hook and attaches it to the dog.

"They've come for Blackie," she says. "I need some peace. You stay here. I don't want them to see you. They live in the country. Blackie will be happier there. He'll be fine. He won't even miss you he'll be so happy. I promise you. He'll be fine."

She guides the frightened dog out the front door, his tail between his legs. Roy watches from the window. A boy his own age is petting his dog, is holding him in his arms, is leading him back to his family's car.

Roy doesn't mean to. He doesn't mean to do a lot of things these days. He shrieks. He shrieks and cries and calls his mother vile names. Bitch, bitch. After shaking the father's hand, his mother retreats from the family's excitement and closes the front door behind her. "What have I done to you," his mother says to him when he will not stop yelling at her. "What have I done to you."

His brother stands in a doorway, silent. The next morning none of them will say any more about it. No one will ever say any more about it. Silence is how they endure.

When, older, Roy reflects on this day he will say, though only to himself, "I don't care how much people say they love you. If they feel they need to hurt you for whatever reason of their own, they will. They will hurt you bad and that's that.

"And everyone will go on living as if it never happened, telling you how much they love you and all the rest of it. And you knowing you must not complain will never say anything either, as if nothing had been broken between you for good. As if love couldn't be as cruel as everything else."

Roy is old enough, his mother agrees, to take the bus to the Port Authority on his own when he wants to. His brother is in college. Mary Sutton is teaching English at a private school in town now. The job is a lot more work, but it pays more money. Jon's education is costing her far more than she can afford. And what about Roy in a few more years? The thought exhausts her.

It's a chilly March morning when Roy steps into Manhattan, happy to be free, completely on his own. He is sitting on a bench in a small park near Hudson Street in the Village when a yelping mutt runs past him, its paws pulpy messes pressing bright red prints onto the pavement. As the dog dashes into traffic, a taxi's tires screech. Roy yells out, "Watch it!"

Having to wait for a light, Roy loses sight of the dog, but follows its bloody tracks to a frantic circle it breaks out of, disappearing near a dock's edge, river bound.

A tug's horn sounds like a howling dog. Roy is cold. He turns back to Twelfth Avenue to cut across an asphalt playground. Two kids rock on a teeter-toter. A third twists the chain on her swing, laughing giddily while she twirls.

The hurt dog has vanished. It's no use to try to find it now.

That night, standing high up behind the balcony at the Met, Roy will hear Mozart's Magic Flute for the first time live. The plot confuses him, but he loves the music when he listens to it on his records. He does not mind how distant the stage is. His ears are keen.

Maybe some things are better not seen too close up, make more sense from far away, Pamina's grief, Tamino's quest, Sarastro's sonorous wisdom, Papageno's silly joy. God listens to Bach but the angels prefer Mozart. A friend he has just met in the high school orchestra, another violin player, had told him that. Maybe so.

4. 1959

He is a counsellor at a camp in the Watchung Mountains when, as
he is coaching a boy's volley ball team, a mangy hound wanders
onto the court from a thick grove of cedar. The boys suspend their
match to look at him.

His ears drag the ground. He is covered with engorged ticks. His
eyes are rheumy and red, his lids swollen. His tail looks broken.

That night, Roy asks the other counsellors for their opinion about
what to do. They all chip in. A day later, the oldest drives him and
the stray to a vet in the nearest town. The stray must stay under
observation over the weekend. When they pick him up, he is free of
parasites, and his eyes are brighter. Soulful eyes, more soulful than
most people's, Roy thinks, and heartbreakingly sad.

He won't name him yet. He is not sure he will be able to keep him.
The dog doesn't like to walk on a leash, resists his new leather collar,
eats little. When he is off leash or unchained, he always heads di-
rectly toward the woods, his stride clumsy, unstable, yet determined.

"Your woods," Roys says to him on the fifth night. "These are your
woods, aren't they, fellow?" The old dog is whimpering. The moon
is almost bright as the sun. There is a path leading to the trees, a
gray, curvy, unpaved lane like a plume of smoke rising from a chim-
ney, thinning near the forest.

Soon it will be full dark. Tall pine, maple, ancient oak, sycamore
line the way. Go in, he says silently to the dog. Walk deeper in this
time. No more suffering. You needn't come back to us for anything.
I promise not to worry. I promise I won't try to save you again.

His professor is almost a cliché of a Latin teacher, rumpled, slovenly, cigarette ash on the lapel of his jacket, white hair uncombed, untrimmed, and flourishing like a weedy garden. They are translating Horace together, this afternoon the seventh poem in the second book of Satires. His desk desk sits on a wooden platform. He gazes down on them, not knowing any of their names, though it is almost the end of the semester. No one much minds. He gives them all A's.

"You will have read the poem to yourselves many times over already of course, Gentlemen, since Horace requires of us moderns great attention," he says. "I need not illuminate you much further save to enlighten you with this anecdote.

"In the latter part of our previous century, a minor scholar, a poetaster as we like to say, by the name of Covington translated the poem we are about to translate together. I will read to you part of what he wrote near its end:

> No company's more hateful than your own
> You dodge and give yourself the slip; you seek
> In bed or in your cups from care to sneak
> In vain: the black dog follows you and hangs
> Close on your flying skirts with hungry fangs.

"The 'black dog follows you.' Strange, isn't it, Gentlemen? I needn't remind you, need I, that there is no 'black dog' in Horace. Some dusky sort of companion, yes, but no black dog.

"How did it roam into Horace's poem then, I ask you, and from where? Churchill's 'black dog,' I suppose we could say. I believe this poem has been attributed as the great man's source. And now it's wandered off, hasn't it, nowhere to be found. Not in Horace's Latin at least."

Professor Woodbridge sets his text down flat on the top of his table-top desk and gazes out the window at the clouds darkening over the campus, more snow predicted for all of Jersey soon. Roy notices, not for the first time, how very old he is, how antiquated.

"I had a black dog once, Gentleman."

Roy could swear later he is talking to him before all the others. But is he? Why should he? He averts his eyes.

"A fine black lab he was, too. He died of advanced age at nearly fifteen." Professor Woodbridge thumps his own chest as if to explain. "A bad ticker. I have never ceased grieving.

"Well. Love, Gentlemen. Cave canem, eh?"

6. 1967

A small dog, poodle-mix, lies in the north bound lane of the town's main drag, run-over or hit. Reckless cars dash past, not trying to drive around it. If not now dead, it soon will be, crushed, its life lost, wantonly destroyed if it isn't rescued at once.

Careless of his own safety, Roy's new boyfriend Alan leaps off the walkway into traffic, picks the dog up, cradles it like a child, and carries it free from danger. A tag reveals a number. Alan dials it on a payphone while the dog licks his cheek.

Once he arrives, its owner maintains he couldn't have known what great harm his dog had just faced, he didn't even know it had scratched through the screen door until he saw the rip, but he is

ashamed of his negligence nonetheless, relieved, hugging it grate-
fully in his arms.

Who is this Alan beside him, Roy wonders as they stand in line
at the box office of the theater showing The Graduate? A man on
an evening walk who who will keep safe what he can. "I love you,
Alan," Roy whispers.

7. 1970

Roy's dog Olive is ill again. She is hurting bad. No one knows how
many days she has left.   No bird, no dog, no man is just a 'thing,'
Roy believes. A soul inhabits all that lives. She still likes to bark
at a jay taking off in flight with no hope of catching it. She loves to
chase squirrels up trees. Roy dreams of his chasing after her, leash-
less, through the night.

She had been abused before Roy adopted her from the pound a cou-
ple of years ago, abandoned, teats distended. She scratches an ear.
Her snout is whiskery grizzled. "Olive," he says. "Pal. Good gal."

If quietly scolded, she'll jump on his bed and cower. She studies
him. Where does he go all day when he leaves his small apartment
and she needs him most? To work? What is work? Pushing papers
at a law office.

Roy steadies himself by recalling the last untroubled day they had
spent together. It was raining. She and he hid under a broadly
spreading sycamore to try to keep dry. A rat scurried by. Olive
tugged on her leash. There was a small furry gray thing to chase.

The wetter the day, the more she likes to test him. More puddles
to try to lap up, tail wagging as she sniffs at gopher holes and the
promise of cats.

Roy is crying. What must Olive think? Does a dog, dreaming, ever regret its life or mourn for the souls it must lose to mere memory?

After she died, Patrick Rice, his boss, said to Roy, "I loved having my Dylan with me every day. Eleven years we were together. I know he forgave me for being who I am."

8. 1972

Vincent lies next to Roy in his bed. After two years in Nam, he had flown home to Brooklyn eighteen months ago. He and Roy met in a bar in the Village. He doesn't talk much about his tour. Tonight is different though. Neither bothers to wonder why. Maybe it's the great grass they have smoked. Probably not.

"We were about a mile from the delta," Vince continues. "Despite the heat and bugs and snakes, home free for a while. In the middle of the jungle, in the midst of nothing but the madness of its vines and thickets and gigantic leaves, we fell upon a clearing and a mess of about fifteen bamboo huts. Fifteen. Jesus Christ.

"But only a few were still standing. The rest had been leveled or burned. All the people who lived there, about forty I guess, were dead. The VC.

"I guess they thought they were informers or spies or simply no use to them and so dangerous. They killed them all, slaughtered them, the kids too, mostly with machetes. They didn't want to waste bullets, the bastards.

"The carnage was awful, the blood, the stink. It made me sick. We burned the bodies that the VC had tried to burn but hadn't managed to, shoveled the ashes into some dirt, buried the rest deeper.

"I don't know. What I can't escape is how I keep seeing, all the time keep thinking that scene must be the cruelest thing anyone should have to see in a life.

"What I don't understand is why the worst of it for me might be this sorry excuse for a dog that had survived the massacre, this emaciated mongrel dog, pawing at one grave, whimpering, with nothing left for it, nowhere to go.

"I looked at it digging and digging and I couldn't quit sobbing. Still can't," Vincent says and lights another joint. Roy moves to hold him. "No. Not just yet," Vince says.

9. *1975*

Roy adopts a new collie. Perversely, pathetically even, no one needs to tell him, he has named him Luke after his lost dog. Luke likes to snuggle next to him in bed, just as the first Luke would, or stretch out by his side when he reads at night.

Sometimes, living alone–though he does not want to, though he dreams of finding a steady partner–in his small apartment over a garage in Jersey City, he thinks he can hear the wind whistling through loose panes. It sounds like a ghosty intruder entering his brain. Listen, his dread instructs him. A key is turning in the lock, the latch clicks, the door opens.

All this he hears time and again, alone at night. Not an intruder. Not a burglar. Only a fantasy. His father is home. He is letting himself in.

New Luke is a strange dog. If Roy lets him out onto the deck, he will stare, stretching his neck, for a half an hour or more at the sky as if he is looking for some particular cloud or star.

If Roy closes a door inside, Luke will bark until he opens it to prove
to him that no one is there. When he turns off the lights to watch
a movie on his TV screen, Luke will gaze back into the dark bed or
bathroom adjacent to the living room as if he smells or sees some-
one inside them, waiting, lurking. Every time Luke does so, Roy
has to check to make sure, to see if he can see what Luke sees, if he
should fear what Luke fears.

Yet every evening when he comes home from work, Luke is waiting
for him behind the door, wagging his tail, licking his face, eager to
assure him all is well.

All is well, Luke. Guardian. Anubis. Seer.

10. 1980

Back in his apartment after spending a long rainy Saturday after-
noon at the Whitney's Edward Hopper Retrospective, Roy wonders
what to make of it all,

recalling the blank faces of Hopper's houses,
the ominous rows of trees,
the lighthouses and barns and bleakly Gothic buildings,

the people always waiting,
waiting in a theater or a restaurant or a rented room,

waiting for something, someone that will likely never come,
who will never appear,
waiting for something important to happen to them,

Roy

sensing something must hover beyond the dark tunnel into which
Hopper's horsemen ride,

beyond the curve by the gas station in a landscape
which deepens as twilight
descends into night.
beyond the dark wall of trees
at the bottom of the stairs and out the door,

Roy

yearning to see
what a bald man,
his age uncertain,
who has just quit raking a patch of lawn sees,
looking up and back
as if towards the source of light
that washes over him,
that pours through the slot or alley
between the stark old houses where he stands,

Roy

needing to see what a nude woman sees,
a woman who
having just gotten out of bed
is holding a cigarette,
not quite in profile,
standing in a shaft of strong morning light
that falls through a window beyond view,

Roy

longing to know what it is a couple sees,
the woman standing,
the man sitting,
outside their clapboard house on the Cape,
their feet hidden in tall brown grass,

above all anxious to know, hoping to see what their dog,

their dog
a collie too,
sees,

startled, its eyes drawn
not toward the black woods at its side,
but out of the painting,

as if he, Roy, could be drawn out of his life as well,

toward light,
the eternal source
of light,
the hidden light
that falls on all
randomly
and is to all who see it clearly,
by light made lucid,
each one in turn,
in their growing astonishment,
in awe

or so Roy imagines, as he remembers it,
the show,
Hopper's paintings one by one,

and the dog, the dog in his favorite of them all,
a collie identical to his Luke,
depicted in a painting,
there,
hanging on the Whitney's walls,

Good Luke, he says back home, patting him on his head. Good boy.

A Revenant's Voices

I— In the Park

It's so peaceful here, isn't it, like being deep in woods. The tulip trees blooming early, resplendent, petals floating in air. It's a Japanese postcard. What a lovely day. Look. A coyote. The third we've seen this morning.

Why didn't he join us? He always has walked with us.

I called him and called him. There was no response.

Disappeared again, has he?

So it seems. Let's circle the pond, what do you say? I love to watch the elderly Chinese ladies performing Tai Chi to the music they play on their little portable radios.

Well, it's not unlike him to vanish for a few days, I suppose. We shouldn't be worried yet.

He's changed. He was livelier not so long ago. Much more fun.

We all were.

Ah, mortality. How it alters everything. Listen. Juncos.

If he hasn't emerged by the end of the week, I think we should pound on his door and demand an answer or two.

All right. Here's a sunny patch where the grass is dry. Let's sit here for a while and rest.

He's a secretive man, our friend.

Imponderable.

A mystery.

An unsolvable one.

Lost. Most of all that. Quite lost.

Perhaps we should worry. He has been acting despondent.
Stand-offish. Do you imagine he could have?

Shshshsh. Hush. Who knows? Look. Over there. A red-tailed
hawk high in that tree feeding its young in its nest.

It is so restful in the park this morning I could lie here all day.

Staring at the sky.

Yes. Just lying here and looking up at the sky forever. Content.

II—Two Notes

1.

If asked, I would admit to you I was a fool. But I wasn't a fool. Just a
boy once.

I believed God would endure like the sun, would last forever, be on
fire always, his light sufficient proof of paradise, no summer blessed
until afternoon lightning had tested July and granted me the joy of it,
had overwhelmed with its violent storms.

When I was ten, I heard a preacher say heaven was a city as dazzling-
ly golden and bejeweled as noontime on the hushed, shallow water
of the Louisiana cypress swamp we lived near. And I believed what
I had heard because I had seen it for myself, that golden light at its
height in the middle of day.

I was a poor swamp boy, crazed by plantation fantasies I thought
must be heaven.

At night, I would lie on my back between rows of sugar cane and
stare through stalks at the Milky Way, its stars twinkling sea-blue or
morning-glory red, meteorites burning as they hurled toward earth,
my first glimpses of God falling from the sky. And I grew afraid.

After my first hurricane, wandering, shelterless, I passed by a
cracked, moss-covered tomb in New Orleans, gaping open. I could
believe the dead might walk again out of such rubble, ghosts who
had to learn a new way to breathe, their bodies battered by rain,
tormented by wind, smothered in mud like my parents.

I would dream of Mary's assumption, how the priests had described
and shown us it in paintings. I could see her flying everywhere like
a bird with no place to light.

I watched the Mississippi inundate gutters, alleys, streets, whole
wards. I saw it pulling down doors, crashing through windows,
overflowing balconies, rooftops, drowning rats, chickens, horses,
gardens, crops, and children young as me.

I was there. I witnessed everything.

And I believed in God all the more fervently because I knew he must
come again like that, with his power unleashed, liberating us from
sin by the flood of his majesty, a steeple–tall wall of water drown-
ing our recalcitrant, stubborn selves, purifying us so that our souls
would not shudder or recoil from our bodies, wicked as they were.

I found signs of the Lord in the relics left behind by those he had
lifted naked to his bosom: a strand of costume pearls, ripped black
jeans, a colored pencil, shards from a cookie jar, two bashed-in
clocks, a battered doll, a boot without a sole, a blade less knife han-
dle, a faded feathered hat, water-sodden hymnals, a knotted neck-
tie, a silt-soiled photo album, a sludge-covered antique trunk.

Each one a sign. Each one an impediment to me. Each one a rem-
nant, a battered icon of a life the water had taken and discarded as
leftover residues of his grace, the men, women, and children he had
taken from the world to claim as his saved.

Remains I saw the river had piled into altars made from silt-soaked
clothes and black pots and yellow beads and bike chains, a girl's
blue bow. Had created out of soggy pages ripped from a dictionary
or a leather bound bible, a locket, a wicker basket, a gym bag with
one sneaker.

I was rummaging as a child would through old toys, through salva-
tion's throwaways.

What is memory but human residue spared for a while from the di-
sasters of time? That desperation of the soul that time leaves behind
in ruined things?

Oh, Lord walking on the Galilee, pacifying every tempest, as a boy
in Louisiana, I believed in you more fervently than any priest I
knew until the days when I witnessed your storms.

Why had I not seen before your hidden face, seen through your
mask of kindness and grace to the wrath concealed behind it?

Yet I will always be, so a long as I live, a foolish kid sitting in a pirogue fishing for bass and blue gills, waiting for God to make things better, to bring us through his glory to our lives' promised peace.

2.

Paradise is this morning's wind blowing the world westward, the ever changing sea and sky.

It is a play enacted by others, its plot unfolding toward some surprising happy ending.

It is these white spumes tossed by wind across the beach while plovers skitter on sand seeking larvae.

It is water flowing through gutters, down drains, across the sand rushing toward the sea with nothing to lose or gain.

It is my mind as it wanders, lost in dreaming dreams of rollers roaring in, of three crows cawing in shrill reply.

I sleep to hurts and wounds, the gulls' cries I hear at night, a flock of them on a long winter journey, restless with despair.

Waves, cloud-muted sun, how mortally cold the Pacific is, how many souls it has undone.

Dear God, let all those who travel unwilling be returned to port, like dreamers back from sleep.

Pleased with themselves, their boards balanced on their heads, surfers stride out of churning water having once more mastered the waves.

A good storm breathes dust back to life, doesn't it? I long for the
next one.

A dog is barking at waves along the beach. I do not want to die
haphazardly as a bit player in an everyday scene. Another dog play-
fully chases its own tail.

Waves crash closer to where I am standing. More crows rummage
though overturned garbage cans. The sea grass rustles. A flock of pel-
icans tips their wings to a sun that is breaking through clouds at last.

Oh precious sunlight. Is any moment known to be true only by
what it endures? Might peace rise out of the sea like love?

My soul is unsure, uneasy, old friends. Why do I believe in any-
thing anymore but this?

Yes, I am runoff flowing over rain-pounded sand toward the ocean,
carrying the sediment of days.

A squall is forming over the horizon, black and billowing. It will
rain hard again soon.

I stand on a dune until, too drenched to stay, until I retreat home to
write you, almost to warn you, dear friends, of the days ahead.

See how storms shape-shift the dunes and beach. And so, this
morning, I say goodbye.

I would not trouble you with this message if God had been proven
to be greater than the sum of his victories, had shown himself as
more than his silence.

Perhaps he has. I must go elsewhere to see.

III— In His Apartment

Let's stop looking for clues. We've found none really, just two scribbled, strange notes that tell us nothing about where he might have gone.

Poor, confused man. I'm terribly worried.

Have you spoken to any of his other friends?

Just one. She's had no word from him and knows less than we do. She's alarmed, too. He's just vanished, she said. Like that, without a sign. For too many days now. Or longer. No one is sure for how long exactly. It could be weeks.

Fortunately he gave us both spare keys.

I think I might have preferred it if he hadn't. I'm uneasy about sneaking in like this, aren't you?

It's not sneaking. We have a right to be here. His permission.

What do you make of what he's written us? His words are a bit alarming now we've read them twice, don't you think?

It's not like him just to leave town, to disappear with no warning whatsoever. I thought I knew him. Apparently no one does.

Should we suspect foul play?

It's implausible.

But possible.

Anything is possible. That does not make it likely.

It is unkind of him to vanish without offering us a reason, just two outrageous notes.

So naked in a way, so fraught with spiritual torment. Do you think we should inform the police? That we should tell someone in authority? Goodbye, he wrote.

In two or three days maybe. There's no need to make a fuss yet Suppose he should return only to discover we all have made this dreadful commotion over him, that we had worried over him like some anxious, too protective mother. Imagine his embarrassment at all the needless excitement and wasted effort because of a simple mistake in judgment, of over interpreting what he wrote us.

Poor man. Poor, poor god-haunted man.

And a priest-haunted child, too, I'd wager. Wouldn't you?

I don't understand it.

Neither do I.

Perhaps we should search his apartment more thoroughly. Look for clues in drawers and closets and under his bed. We've only explored the surface.

Let's wait.

For how long?

I don't know. I have faith.

In what?

Not in what he wrote us, certainly. That's quite loony. But, underneath it all, he is a sensible man, isn't he, plain spoken and clear-headed if a bit shy about revealing what is on his mind? Good sense always wins out in the end, doesn't it?

Rarely.

Then tell me. What else might we do? Pray? Please offer a better idea.

I can't.

No one can. It's what makes life so confusing if you think about it too much. No one has offered a better solution to our sufferings. Not anyone down through human history. Pray, they say. And it never works.

IV—Two Letters

1.

Today I have set sail on the Mediterranean sea. Blue sky, bronze sun, white sand sparkling where the winds blow fiercest. I am on an odyssey toward my true home on an island no one can find on chart or map.   Not even I know where it is.

Our captain smiles at his crew. We passengers grin back. We have departed our final port. No one fears voyaging too far out.

This morning, the sea reddens as dawn rises over the a Greek island's mountains.

Dozing in my hammock, I can see dead men rising out of the placid water.

I can hear our boat rocking, waves lapping against the hull so gently they lull me deeper into sleep, into dreams enticing me back to harbor, to the old gods men have erected in statues, façades, columns.

When becalmed, we wait, our ship precariously placed at the edge of all things, like a vase set on a table that the slightest trembling

might make fall. I remember the city of Ys drowning in its fable. I
recall Poe's story of the maelstrom. Name me the name of a sane
man surviving at the bottom of a whirlpool.

Suspended between sea and sky, waiting for dawn on the deck of a
ship in a painted landscape, my spirit is untroubled, peaceful and
quiet.

It is the God within God who resides in human unknowing, in the
silence unheard in the troughs between waves, it is the God within
God I believe in now.

It is he who will save me, my friends.

2.

I believe in these days, never doubt the journey as I sail onward to-
ward death just as I knew in my youth to trust my father oaring our
boat on the bayous.

Beyond earth's end, past every horizon, beyond the galaxies, God
waits for me. After hope dies, after I have reached the nowhere I
travel to on invisible, open seas, I will return to you.

Tonight, in the chill air, the ship's lights flare yellow on white waves
like ignes fatui, their flames flickering as if set there by design.

The sun's long afterglow beckons me to consolations that might be
no more than shadows. But why should I mind if it is an illusion
that rows me? Why should I care if it is phantom disguised as my
death that has seized the oars.

On my earliest birthdays, my father lit so many extra candles on
my cake I thought our house would be set ablaze by his folly, by his
need to find gestures to show me how much he loved me. The folly
of loving anything, anyone so much more than one can.

We know God by the exuberance of his kindness, by the excesses of a love we thought we should fear, by how his light breaks suddenly over the Cyclades.

As a boy, I watched a winter twilight descending through longleaf pine. I saw dawn rising over the bayou. I stared blindly into a noon sun mirrored by silt darkened waters. Anxious intimations, those illuminations of a God who courses through each day a child lives for if left unharmed.

Look with me, friends, at how a ship's lights turn water into fire, the Pleiades reflected by the sea.

The seductions of wonder.

The promises resounding in everyday joys.

The silence foredooming us we've heard while waking to the voices of an ordinary morning.

Friends, do not fret. Do not search for me. Be at ease.

The ancient sea where I wait for you to join me someday is clearest blue. I stand on the opposite shore from you, beckoning. Follow me.

The Lord preaches to the sea. Paradise, he admonishes.

Paradise.

It's a happy day when you were reborn from dust, ash, and clay.
So may this vision be true, my gift to the world, no fantasy but souls playing sunning dancing loving.

Your soul is your body redeemed. Your spirit is your flesh intensified.

Be content. Know pleasure. Know peace.

You, who stay by my side to celebrate with me my miracles of silence, sing abandonment, sing madness, sing faith.

Sing imagination.

Sing paradise with me.

V—In a Restaurant

Now that you brought it up, he does seem much better. Calmer. Less excitable.

Yes, almost back to normal, I'd say. This is excellent chicken, by the way.

Yes. So is the halibut. Perfection.

Excellent wine, as well, expertly ordered.

Thank you.

You invited him to join you last Sunday at this same restaurant, didn't you? How is he in public? All right? He hasn't seemed to want to join me away from his apartment just yet. He did cook me quite a pleasant meal the other evening though.

Subdued. Quiet. He spoke very little. Answered a few questions. Nothing important. Good appetite. Quite reasonable in his speech, I'd say. Not hallucinating, though sometimes, rarely, it is a bit hard to tell. Otherwise rational.

He's never been much of a talker has he? Unlike us, two chatterboxes.

Someone has to do the listening.

How did he look to you all these months after?

Gaunt. Pale. But, as I said, sane. When I asked him where he'd been hiding all those weeks while we were both so worried about him, he said Greece. He still claims it was Greece.   I was alarmed for a moment. If I had asked to see his passport or some other proof, he wouldn't have been able to show me anything, of course. I didn't want to rattle him again. I've decided he must mean it as a metaphor.

For what? For his madness?

No. For his peace of mind. He thought he had found it there.

Our friend. The Amazing Vanishing Man. I wouldn't call what he found peace.

It wasn't an act. He wanted to come back from wherever he was.

Of course he did. I'm sorry.

He really did disappear inside himself. He still has brief visions, he says. Little episodes. He probably always will, from time to time. He doesn't complain about it. Nor do I think he welcomes them any-more. But who knows for sure?

A frightening prospect, those visits. Never knowing when some deity might appear out of nowhere. Never knowing when you might be hit by another bolt of cosmic lightning.

I couldn't bear it. Should we order dessert now or wait until lat-er, after we've finished the wine?

After. I'd prefer to delay the pleasure a bit. My dish was so rich-
ly sauced. Excessive.

But a gateau basque? Custard? Brandied cherries? How can that
temptation not goad you into action?

Everything delicious tempts me. Every tantalizing pleasure.

Such wanton hedonists we are. Both of us.

He's a mysterious man, our friend.

Determined to keep his secrets secret.

What a peculiar childhood he seems to have had.

He intimated to me that he regrets having written us all those notes
and letters. Wild nonsense, he calls them now. Yet once or twice,
while I was speaking, he appeared to be distracted by something.
Folly. folly, he kept saying, as if he had caught a glimpse of some-
thing quite, well, foreign to us. Then the cloud would pass.

Right. When I saw him a few days ago, his eyes for a while seemed
unable to focus on anything stable. He kept looking around like
someone searching for the exits, for some way to escape. I can't say
I'd blame him for trying.

He must feel frightened, terrified by what's happened to him, what-
ever that was, wherever he went in his spirit, I mean.

Where do you guess he really went, if he did go somewhere real and
geographic?

I suspect to a cabin he's rented before in the north of Mendocino. My
hunch is that while he was going through whatever he was suffering

he preferred to be completely alone. He saw it coming and left just in time.

Does he still talk to you about God?

Of course. Doesn't he with you?

Lowering his voice, almost as if whispering a confidence, he remarked the other day, Nothing else matters to me, it never did, not since I was little. I only care about faith. I want to believe in something. Something real. Then he thought better of having said it and looked away. I didn't pursue it.

He fears everyone misconstrues what happened to him. He believes we all think he had gone slightly mad for a few weeks.

Which is probably true, wouldn't you agree?

But he is recovering bravely, isn't he? If he were here, I would applaud him.

And so embarrass him.

Undoubtedly. That dish we shared was quite special. Yes, an amazing sauce. Delicate and rich.

A touch of sherry added to the cream, I think.

I do find him a bit harder to take these days, don't you?

He's still quite likable most of the time.

Oh, I very much consider him a close friend still, no matter what.

So do I. A lonely man, our friend, all in all. It's too bad about the touch of madness in him, of course.

Solitary. Reclusive. Call him what you will.

His frightful moodiness bothers me at times. Do order the gratin next time. I've never tasted better.

I will. I promise. Well, at least whatever did happen to him, wherever he did go, it's nearly over. He's almost out of danger.

Time is the great healer, they say. Excuse me for asking this. But don't you ever think about our lives? Question them? What they've become?

Do you want to know what I really think? I think an ordinary life like mine or yours without any meaning to it at all is much harder to live than one devoted to any God, whichever one you might choose. Yet we manage somehow. We get on with our lives without having to turn them into tragedy or the rites of a church or some mindless meditative practice. We never have to overreach or strain beyond our ken. What a lot of nonsense he put down on paper for us to read. What a lot of foolishness he talked. And now surely he's ashamed of it. He must be. I don't care what he might feel, what he claims to have experienced, whether the heights of joy or the lows of despair. Lord, spare me such pointless torment.

Is it always pointless? I wonder.

Wonder? Whatever for? What about? Why are you shaking your head back and forth like that?

Am I? It's just that.

Go ahead. Don't be ashamed. Tell me.

It's just that sometimes I don't want to be myself. I don't want to
be like this, like us.   Deep down, I long for something more, some-
thing deeper or more real or permanent, don't you? I don't want his
pain. Heavens, no. I couldn't bear that suffering. But I can't stand
things as they are. This world as it is. I envy him.

Some Ways They Mourn

1.

Like spilled oil on a wet asphalt road, red, gold, and blue rings halo
the moon. He peers through a window. Slumped in her wingback
chair, his mother is clutching her left hand to her bosom, her glass-
es crooked on her nose. His father is watching the ten o'clock news
with the sound off.

Moths around their porch light whir like bees swarming about a
hive. Slugs have left a trail of slime across the walkway. Joe crush-
es a beetle inching up the front door screen and flicks its mashed
carcass into a shrub.

A breeze rattles the spindly dogwood branches. The sweet min-
gled smells of gardenia and japonica tickle his nose. The next door
neighbor's Rott barks at his mother's roaming cat, always wander-
ing off. Jeanne has promised to adopt it, but he will have to catch it
first. Bats swoop through the oaks in the side of the yard.

He can't go in yet. He must wait a while longer, hoping to find what
he needs to say, how much to tell them of what is true. That it is
long past time for them to leave their house and live in the Method-
ist Home, tomorrow the dreaded day.

Indecisive, reluctant just to walk in on them as he did yesterday, Joe
jumps the gulch that borders the woods behind the backyard and
crosses a meadow to the abandoned pasture that had been turned
into a football field for kids to play in when he and Tommy were
boys. Now milkweed, sumac, and goldenrod grow hay high all over
it. Sticking to his slacks, burrs prick his skin.

A pickup brakes near a curve in the road. Moving too fast, swerving,
it skids close to where a goal post had stood and halts on the

135

shoulder. Along sidelines marked by heavy flat stones he had raced past to score a touchdown in a moment of glory no one else could recall anymore, not his father, mother, or younger brother, not even Jeanne, that day long ago, the four of them cheering him on.

The pickup turns off its headlights and drives away in the dark. Why? Goodbye is what Joe needs to find some way to say. Goodbye to his parents' old life. Goodbye to his own life some day, too. Isn't that what everyone must learn how to do? To say goodbye to it all?

2.

In the morning, his sister is shooing her older daughter off to high school, a kerchief tied round her hair, her blouse tucked into her faded jeans, her hands protected by leather work gloves. Jeanne waters her rows of red and yellow tulips that are blooming in front of a just pruned backdrop of pink and white azalea. From his car, hidden by trees, Joe watches her chop the soil or knock earth off weeds' roots before she tosses them into an old sheet she will use to haul them to the mulch pile in back.

Pausing, she sees Joe approaching her on the driveway and wipes a glove across her flushed, sweaty brow. "Hello again, Joe," she says, frowning. "I guess I know why you're here. Today's the big day."

"Yes," he says, "sorry to bother you, Jeanne." He doesn't kiss her cheek but shakes her hand. "I'm driving them to the home later this afternoon. Everything's already packed. The workmen arrived just after dawn, right on schedule."

"Yes. I know. Mother called. Desperate, I'd say."

"I thought she might. It would be nice of you to stop by before they leave at three or four. Just to wish them well. Cushion the blow a little maybe."

136

"No can do, Joey." She shakes her head. "I haven't got the time.
The girls you know. Their hectic schedule. I'll visit them after
they've settled in. If not tomorrow, the next day. I promise. After
you've gone. I do try to visit them once a week, you know. I have
for years."

"Yes, I do know. And am grateful to you for it. I do know it's been
rough on you. Your life is so busy. Don't be bitter, Jeanne."

"I'm not. Nor do I deserve that scowl I think I see you making
without meaning to, Joe. You're the one that left, after all, you and
Tommy. I'm the one that stayed. I'm the one that had to stay."

"I thought you and Mark and your girls were happy."

"We are happy. That's not what I mean. Forget it. I've got a lot to
do before Mark gets home tonight, Joe. It's been good to see you.
Next time, if there is a next time, try to visit a little longer. But
right now I have a garden to improve before I head off for work.
Call me some time. It would be nice to talk. I'll let you know how
they're doing. I promise. O.K.?"

"Sure, Jeanne," Joe says, watching a purple finch perched on a
bobbing stem clamping its beak on a fat berry. Their feathers bright
from a morning shower under Jeanne's watering hose fanning the
lawn, two cardinals squabble in an ancient hickory tree.

Why is Jeanne so red-faced as she turns away? Why does she so
angrily resume her gardening? Why is she watering her yard when
there's been so much rain? His sister has always puzzled him. He
would like to have known for himself the happiness she claims
as hers but can't ever seem to find it in Jeanne beyond her anger
toward him. Walking back to his car, he checks his cell phone. The
movers have left two starred messages he won't listen to. He knows
exactly how late he is.

3.

So this is what is left of our home, he says to himself after he had
driven his parents to their new residence and himself back to the
house for one more look at what remains behind: just things as-
sembled, waiting for the van, crammed together in the living room.
A cane chair, wicker rocker, pine hutch, cupboard, knickknack
stand, cedar chest. Two green wine bottle lamps. Three needlepoint
pictures. A dining table. Boxes piled on boxes of silverware and
plates and cups and glasses and crockery, all wrapped in newspaper.
A leather sofa. Five standing lamps. Suits and dresses on hangers
draped over a coffee table. Unpolished shoes. Empty luggage. A
trunk stuffed with old magazines and books. Decorated porcelain
dishes meant for display on a wall. A china service for guests. Crys-
tal for Sundays. Old toys from their childhood. An electric train. A
Monopoly set. Decks of cards. A hand woven afghan. Three com-
forters smelling of must. A telescope. Two fishing rods.

Things, dead things waiting for men from the auction house to haul
it all downtown for a one day sale unscheduled as yet, but promised
sometime in the near future. Joe has been assured no one from the
family need be there for it. What doesn't sell will be tossed in the
county junkyard. The check for any profits will be made out and
mailed to his father who won't know what to do with it.

4.

In the back of the Methodist Home, his father sits next to his son
on an iron bench, an uncharacteristic ball cap on his head, his skin
cracked and sandy yellow. A spot of drool dribbles off his cheek.
Joe wipes it away, cleaning up what he had already spilled onto his
neck and undershirt, too. His father, Robert Connick, always needs
to blow his nose these days.

138

All his life he's been called Robert, never Bob. Not once ever Bob. How is it Joe has never learned why? It has never bothered him before. It troubles him this afternoon.

His father closes his eyes. Tears trickle down his cheek. A new thing for Joe to see, then, his father crying.

They are waiting for his room to be prepared for him, the two of them resting side by side, closer than most times before, son and father under a cherry tree. Sparrows and robins hop about and peck the well-kept ground. His father dabs at his eyes with a hand-kerchief. When a maple tree drops its winged seeds into his lap, his fingers play with them.

He starts to wheeze. Inside the building, as a clock chimes five, bells ring. "I'm tired, Joey," his father says. "I'm always tired these days. Worn out."

"The bell's only a signal it's dinner time, Dad. Your room should be available soon. I don't know what's taking the maids so long. Let me check."

"No, no," his father says. "Don't bother. It'll never be right for me anyway, Joe. This life here, I mean. My mind's not right some-times, they tell me. I'm not so sure. You know what I'm saying? I'm bored most of the time. Aren't you?"

5.

Green is his mother's favorite color. Lime green or grape green or avocado. It doesn't matter if it is that precise, that exact a choice, of course. But the green of her room, one flight up and two halls down from her husband's, upsets her, makes her anxious, especially the violent greens of the chintz pillows and curtains and flowery wallpaper. It's all wrong. "It looks like the lime sherbet and ginger ale, that awful concoction, I used to have to serve at church events," she'd complained at once to the chief administrator, appealing to him for another room. "Well if I have to live here, I might as well get used to it," she says to her son, "I suppose I'm to make the best of it. But what a nuisance it is. What nonsense."

Joe drums his fingers on a bedside table. He is ashamed of himself for being so eager to leave. His mother's favorite family photograph rests propped on a swatch of apple green lace on the oak dresser next to it. Jeanne's careful pose shows off her lovely nose, swan neck and fine cheekbones. Joe is standing behind her, the only one not smiling, looking boldly toward the camera in his best dress suit. But Tom, Tommy sits between their mother and father in pride of place, a peace symbol displayed on a big, almost garish lapel pin, his long straight blond hair flowing down to his shoulders.

Not gay exactly but a pilgrim Tom had informed them all the night of his twenty first birthday, just a day before that family portrait was taken thirty years ago. And, with surprising ease, Elizabeth had responded, "A pilgrim, dear? Then you must go from here. You must do whatever it is you need to do, go wherever you need to go, to be happy. I mean with our blessing, too, yes, Robert?" To which proposal his father had readily, if grumpily agreed. Was it really that easy?

Joe holds its frame tighter, fearful he might drop the picture, break-ing the glass, or crazily toss it across the room. He felt cheated by it, by the joys and comforts it implied they'd known. And what if they had and he hadn't or hadn't noticed that he had been happy, after all? But no. Life doesn't work like that.

"I miss him," his mother whispers from the bed where she has been lying down for an hour or so to test its comfort, to discover whether it would succeed better than her own in letting her sleep. "I miss

Tommy. I miss that boy so much. Forgive me, Joe. But I do. I can't help how much. I just do."

"So do I," Joe says, putting the picture back on the dresser exactly where he had found it, his mother still observant of, vigilant about such niceties, the kindness of respecting that something belongs where she has put it. A bell rings again throughout the building, alerting the residents it is last call for supper.

"I still don't know why he had to die, do you? So young, so handsome," his mother says, gazing out the window where night is just beginning to form, as ideas form in her head these days, she confides in him as if it were meant to be a secret.

"No," Joe says. "I guess nobody ever will know why. Not me, that's for certain."

"So young. I won't be able to live here, you know," his mother says, shaking her head. "I'll never be able to live here without your father beside me in the same room, snoring all night long."

"He walks in his sleep, Mother. He wanders."

"Yes. It is what some old folks do for lack of something better. When they are left too much alone," his mother says, grinning, almost smiling as she would smile in long lost days whenever she said something slightly off color or risqué. "Me, I just imagine myself pretty again, flirting with your father."

<h3 style="text-align:center">6.</h3>

The next day, the house on Henderson Road where his parents lived all of their life together stands completely empty, stripped, bare, ready for sale. Like a ghost himself, Joe passes through it one last time, walking through door after door, room after room, down hall after hall as if he were exploring the darkness everywhere inside it now like someone holding a flame inside a cave, desperately hoping to find the opening where he'd entered it, some way to get free, back to daylight.

He steps outside to listen to the locusts' droning, the frogs' croaking, to breathe in the sweet smell of honeysuckle and magnolia dripping in the air. He feels dizzy, his senses confused, too much emotion swirling inside him, too much to think about at once.

Can two people ever know the same thing, the same past? What is memory if not that promise? Would he and Tom, say, or he and his mother have remembered these smells, these sounds around their house, those walls and beams and ceilings inside it, could they have ever recalled them, cherished them in the same way, together?   If not, if each of us is lost in himself, then what is love for?

He abandons the porch and circles the pine grove to his car in the driveway. A need to sob pierces his gut, but he tightens his muscles, grabbing an oak branch to steady himself.

His mother is undressing him, slipping on a night shirt, carrying him in her arms to his bed. Tom is not yet born. He vows to her he never sleeps. She kisses him and says, "Joey, you're only confusing life with your dreams. You won't when you're older. Don't worry."

And he didn't, he thinks it might be true to say, he didn't worry for a whole week just that once.

7.

As he drives to the airport, the trees along the road arch into a tunnel, all of them webbed with caterpillar tents, their trunks and branches covered with lichen and moss. Thickets of wild roses bloom off the shoulders, their colors brightening wherever twilight breaks through the canopy.

The summer he died, able to stand up on his own only by gripping
the back of a chair, staring out the window of the bedroom they had
shared when boys, admiring as he always had the tangled profusion
of the wildflowers growing in a clearing of the woods that began
less than thirty yards behind their home, rapidly going blind, Tom
had said, "Look at it, Joe. Such excess is heaven, isn't it? Like sex.
Glorious. The face of God."

8.

Distant thunder rumbles across the sky. He hopes his redeye flight
won't be delayed too long. Whatever the weather here tonight or
the next day or all the years after he has left it might be like, that he
might read about in the newspaper or see on TV, tomorrow he'll be
back in sunny L.A., fixing lousy scripts he's well paid for in the bun-
galow he owns and lives in alone in the Hollywood Hills. It needs
lots of restoring still, new roof beams and shingles, replacing the
wiring, replanting a garden he has let fall to weeds, cementing back
loose stones on the remodeled porch.

He will return home, of course, since 'home' seems to be what he
must call it. To visit his parents. To see Jeanne and her family.

It is his home, isn't it? At least it was. It is home. Is, was. A prob-
lem that is only a question of tenses and, like the rest of life, unsolv-
able.

The rented car's tires whirr on the wet highway. A chill wind howls
past the window he's cracked open. Together, they make a high-
pitched distant cry, wires buzzing, a white noise ringing in his ears.
Who are you, Joe Connick? Always leaving someplace, always wav-
ing goodbye to some one. The lives of others abide in you for good,
it is saying, You have botched it all, Joe. You have wasted your life.

He slows down. He rolls up the windows. He turns the radio on
loud. Nothing silences it. Nothing. That droning voice.

For a second, no longer, he does what he can't bear to do anymore.
Look at himself. In the rearview mirror, he glances at the ragged,
three inch scar on his right cheek left from a fight he had started
and lost with a guy who had bullied Tom when they were teens and
gouged Joe as he lay beneath him, beaten, with the sharp silver
buckle of his own belt.

And that is it. That is the truth of it. Of life. Only the wounds and
its scars. Only the pain remains.

As he nears the airport, the river running under the bridge on the
highway has grown lazily fatter from so much rainwater spilling
into it since he'd arrived. As he slows for the ramp, the massive
hulk of a black bull waits by a fence to watch him drive past, then,
almost gracefully, weightlessly ambles off.

The last of today's sun is slowly overpowering the dark, scattering
clouds. The runway will be clear on time for him to leave on the
flight he had scheduled. Six hours in the air, as if loosed from his
dream of a life, suspended, going nowhere. Joe is glad of it.

Old Man and Boy (for Gerald Coble)

The late fall wind blows fierce as winter. The sun as it rises is a fire
ball penetrating smoke. Ice-slick from sand, the highway is closed
to traffic. Worn-out clothes, a mattress, its springs exposed, a sofa
with its cushions' stuffing falling out, a shattered chest of drawers
litter a curb, piled at a crosswalk. The air smells of ash, the sea of
fish and crab like the deck of a fishing boat. It is low tide. As the
old man walks by the ocean where the wet sand leaves traces of his
footsteps, the boy he was holds his hand and, gripping it tighter,
pleads, "Don't lose me. Don't let me go."

The old man walks half a block east on the median between the
north and south routes of The Great Highway. Sprawled on a
bench, a man in wine-soaked, grimy clothes is feeding gulls from
a crumpled box of corn cereal. His hands and forearms are black
from crud, his fingernails filthy. On the road, a motorcyclist guns
his engine. On the path, a kid on a bicycle races past. Pony tails
tied in bright red ribbons, two young women in sweat clothes dash
around him. The homeless man shoves a fist of chips into his
mouth, coughs, chokes, wheezes, and spits them out. What has the
old man ever selflessly given? His life is nearly through. He says to
the boy, "I cannot bear myself."

His aunt curls like a cat on her sofa bed, the tumor in her jaw bulg-
ing white as a tennis ball. He reads aloud to her, covers her with a
quilt when she falls asleep. A gust of wind rustles curtains, blows
out candles he lit like incense. The cover of a garbage can waiting
for the trash to be picked up crashes onto the sidewalk. His aunt in
her dying smells of cat. Tomorrow, when he wakes, perhaps she'll
have leaped out a window like her last Siamese to catch in its teeth
a sparrow or somehow a wren to drop by his feet. Look, boy, he
says, pointing at the dead bird some strange cat dropped last night
into his dreams as a token of her love.

The pool is the cool, watery blue of his father's eyes. He watches his
daddy dive in. Breaking free of his mother's grip, the boy darts to
the edge, leaps in after him, and, no swimmer yet, sinks. Where's
bottom? Find it. Swim, swim. The water is colder than water
from a well, darker than night outside his window when the light
is turned off. His father wraps him in a towel, gently holds him,
repeating his silly pet name. Pencil dots, ink spots splotch the sky,
the sun too yellow in his eyes. What does the old man want? To be
saved? "Do what I did," the boy dares him. "Dive in."

The car crawls round each curve, slow as a slug. Having misread
the map, his mother's driving up a steep grade to Hanging Rock
Lake, the road winding between cliff and precipice. The old man
sees the boy's face in the mirror daring him to look. At an instant's
crazy impulse, a bit of excess pressure on the peddle or a turn of
the wheel, she could kill them both. Oblivion in less than a sec-
ond. Anxiety is the fear that endures. Standing at the edge of a
bluff looking over the ruins of the Sutro Baths, he hears the boy cry,
"Why not? Why not jump?"

"Imagine what a life would look life if a man could remake it and be
forgiven," the boy says to him. What has he done to be so judged?
The water is too rough for surfers today. Even the plovers are wary
of skittering too close to the ocean's edge. Stiff as decoys, pelicans
peer down from the dunes. Each propped on a single leg, sand-
erlings stare at the sea. On the ocean walk, elderly Chinese lades
perform, beautiful as ballet, their daily graceful ancient tai chi.
What does it mean for the day he might die, the failure to make life
as lovely?

The boy squeezes through scrub to the sandy clay bank where a
creek empties into the lake. Jagged pebbles and round, slick stones
lie scattered on the water's shallow bed. He takes off his shoes and
socks and walks into the stream, letting it trickle around his ankles.
The water is calm on a windless morning. Skaters dart, zigzagging,
over the surface. Near the bank, a solitary backswimmer waits for its

prey. Distant threads of cloud wind their slow, sinuous way upward to disappear, dissolving, into the purer air above. The boy tugs on some mayweed and queen anne's lace growing along the shore and wades into the lake. He glances back. The old man follows him in, drawn by his smile, the assurance of joy.

Tomorrow is church. The night is moonless. Out of the boy's sight, his friend Tommy Gold strips to his briefs on the dock. Not a house's window or a street light shines on them. The boy undresses. They lie on the beach, side by side. Tommy's body lights a fire in his eyes. Love so seen realizes everything. Back home, frantic moths, scratching beetles, buzzing locust struggle against or cling to his bedroom's window's screens. The old man hesitates to tell the boy what he can't see and won't believe. This night will never happen again. This exact happiness.

His father and the boy rake their lawn clean of wind-torn leaves and needles, pick up downed limbs, twigs, and cones, heap them in a pile by the driveway curb, dowse it with kerosene, toss matches on it, and watch it burn. The flames crackle, spit, sputter, catch at last, leap out of control into a bonfire. Sparks fly free, die into ash, float higher on a warming draft. The burning resin smolders tar-black like blisters of road asphalt. The charred breeze smells like a long leaf pine he saw struck by lightning burning inside for minutes before any obvious part of it, needles or limbs or bark, was consumed. The burning bush, the boy thought. A sign, the old man reminds him, the flame that stays behind after consummation.

On the beach, storms reveal the hull of an ancient shipwreck, nothing left of it except fragments of a bow and stern, blackened wood shards and crusts of rusted metal poking out of the sand. Its fleshless hull is just an outline, like bone bits from a whale. Who watched from what distant shore its crew drown a hundred and fifty years ago? Waves wash over the wreck, freeing more of it. It might be rising out of the sand, preparing to voyage once more. A man's past is like that, the old man says to the boy. It won't stay dead. It wants to be itself again. It wants to sail away.

The old man surveys the tide. The currents are strong. Surfers paddle out, bob in the waves, ride in, risking the power of the rips. The sea as meditation. "Watch me," the boy says bodysurfing the Carolina's coast's wide shelf, tumbling over and over near the shore where the waves gain force, never afraid, ready for the rush of the next trip back in. The waves are loud. The sea as savior. "Lie by my side, Davy," the boy says to the kid he just met outside the beer joint in Ocean Drive, like him too young to go in. "Take off your shoes, your jeans, t-shirt, shorts. Let me muss your hair, lick your skin. Just tonight," the boy says. "All right," Davy replies with a cool guy's grin. "I will." I will, the old man hears again. How he envies whatever time spares. The sea as desire.

An ocean liner is departing dock. Tug boats, barges make way for it. His grandfather takes his hand as the boy crosses the Hudson for the first time, the wind so briny it makes his eyes cry. On the other side, Cinderella at Radio City, a meal at Luchow's, museums, Manhattan. His grandfather wears a black bowler hat and a great coat that droops to his shoes. His leather-gloved fingers hold him tight. Choppy high waves pound the side of the ferry. The boat dips and rocks. Though his grandpa slips and nearly falls, not once during all these absent years has he released his grip, his hold on the old man, or let what he gave the boy go.

A steady, secret creek, jonquils, ivy, dogwood, honeysuckle, a gentle summer rain, an August paradise, the sky vast, warm and good, sweet corn taller than he is in the fields he trespasses over on his way to the lake, chipmunks, fat squirrels being teased by crows where he, the old man, outcasts into solitude from a lonelier childhood, lie on grass in an unsurpassed peace. A warm wind blowing past pleases their bodies like a lover's touch in the aftermath of bliss. "How old are you now?" the boy asks the old man, no date on the calendar able to mark it.

A dangerous west wind rages in. The rain is torrential. Char-gray, smoke-black clouds soar, spiral, and whorl. The ocean is lichen colored or the hue of gray moss on bark. Birds whirl as if caught in a twister, break free, find whatever gust they can use to fly back to land. The old man mourns for the memorial to an unknown man who drowned built out of rocks and shells and pebbles that stood for two days unharmed until the sea swallowed it in yesterday's storms that paved the beach smooth and firm as cement. In the downpour, wherever he looks, he sees what is missing, the boy he was, what time gave and took, found and lost. At the end of the pathway home, he feels the need to say good-bye to the boy, embracing, as shades must: by bidding farewell before fading away, each trying to forgive the other for failing him.

"Boy," he says to himself. "Kid." Thank heaven he is still here. Must he really let him go? Just watch him walk off, climbing the dunes too fast to chase after like a ghost who wanders up and down the coast searching for some precious thing he's lost in the sand? Perhaps they'll meet again some day. Reality is never the same the second time lived. The boy looks back, dashes down to the Pacific's edge, wades in, unafraid of the tide's coming in or of being dragged into its ferocious currents, turns around, and beckons the old man to join him, despite the cold currents, for one last swim. Oh, memory. The sea of it, the shoreless sea they plunge into together.

A Zurbaran at the Cleveland Museum

Zurbaran painted him as if he had already guessed he would become a man stretched out in a crypt emptied of sense some day, a young man in a dazzling white shroud scented with funereal spices and myrrh.

Do people make art to quiet humanity's fears, sing psalms of praise or joy, lament, mourn, find forms for its mute desolations?

I pace in a room stripped bare as his boyhood is in the painting, stare at raw canvas as at a barred door my disbelief has imprisoned me behind.

So I begin exploring the artist's work in the disquiet of no expectation, no sign promised me, the only faith I can see by like an empty space blinding me silent as if it were a blank white canvas I gazed at.

You must know what I mean, you who are reading my words all these years after me, the icons I no longer believed are now yours to see by if you choose to.

Notice how the boy's hair, his slender arms glitter with sawdust, his eyes like a bird's, blackly wary. A fiery cloud looms over his head.

His workroom is dark as a thicket, as a cave shadowed by vines, dank as a tomb. Jewel-like vials, thick books rest on a plain table.

What passion burns in the heart of every child? What rite, night-lit like Good Friday, does each consecrate while playing without fear if lucky enough to be brought into a world that lets them be carefree?

Look with me. Her son has pricked his finger on a thorn from rose
twigs he has woven into a headdress like the bloodied crown he will
wear on Golgotha.

This is the son Mary knows she will outlive and must one day
mourn for and so we with her, we, too, survivors of his death.

I remember a boy, a good friend, who died at twelve, his eyes when
I last saw him astonished by what he had seen and knew so young.

I have witnessed in many mothers' eyes such sorrow. The fate her
son was born for, the child, the life she bore she would ask mercy to
die for.

Mercy, her thorn yours, Lord, whose soul I pray you to possess.

I Thought It Had Stood from Everlasting to Everlasting

1.

The year is turning. A hard wind blows the crows
and gulls in the loops of a Chinese ribbon dance.

Or if they flap their wings, test their strength
against the air's, they fly nowhere, suspended.

All is beautiful, what stays or goes, the waves' white
water tumbling to the sea's tympanic rhythm

that like desire loves itself and in its pulse,
its steady beat, repeats: This never changes.

2.

Antigone knows for the dead any deed done
must be holy, must leave its sacred mark.

Creon chose city over awe and so he wails:
fate, not their own hands, struck down wife and son.

What is lovely to the gods is piety. Yet they stab,
they hang, and make a bridal bed a grave.

3.

Nails driven in, a spear, the Roman soldiers' apathy,
his mother's tears, a restive crowd, agony.

Torture by the Tiberian book: a cross for Jesus,
no broken temple, no noontime dark, no thunder.

His father won't watch, is shocked, hides in horror
at what he's done to his son, betrayed, entombed, decaying.

4.

Annihilation is absurd, death is obscene, sears
all sense. The gods know holy bodies rot to bone.

Yet, dead when their caves are unsealed, Antigone,
Jesus rise in their stories. Legends. Myths.

Poems of what the world is like, the tragedy of wind,
how it blows all away, its force too strong to resist,

and of birds, playing in the air, making a game
of a stormy day, elated by the currents they ride on.

Afterword: Wright Morris

Boy

All there is to see is far away, infinite as ocean
or heaven, frightening him like a boy lost
overboard staring and staring, desperate
to spot a ship. The trees here are bare
as mail boxes, spare as the poles they perch on.
He has chores to perform, gather eggs, chip shit
off chicken wire. A train passing through scratches
a smudged pencil line across the horizon.
Wearing a denim jacket striped like a prisoner's,
his old man is stooped, oppressed by a light
that is cloud heavy in a cloudless sky. The barn
he disappears into is black as a storm cellar.
The boy calls after him. The sun sharpens his broad-
shouldered shadow. He squints to test his eyes.

Traveler

The garden where the blind roamed was walled
for their safety, no danger in smelling scents,
touching petals unstirred by wind. The roses
were pruned to remove all thorns, the slate walkway
square. So Viennese. So European. Like the man
he met who chose to wear a woman's clothes
to pacify his violence in a transvestite calm,
serene, free from feeling, from harm and harming.
Novelties he witnessed abroad between the wars,
though the prairie's winds still blew through
him, creaking swings, slamming shutters against
walls, tumbleweed crackling like fireballs over
a cracked earth stricken by drought, shaking shades
drawn on windows it was far too hot inside to close.

Artist

Open one drawer. A pocket watch, its crystal
broken, match book, two bullets, a chain,
a medicine box, a prescription, its ink
blurred and faded, three nickels, two pennies.
Open another. Paper liner from a time long
before: knives, forks, spoons, workaday,
pewter-gray utensils stacked in rows once
orderly, now crossed like fallen pick-up sticks.
A curtain between rooms is thin as an ancient
wedding veil, a rocker barely visible behind
the lace, brass tacks securing its upholstery.
An oval mirror reflects the knob on a door.
No one is at home. Just things. Life's evidence.
An old clock stuck at five after. An antique lamp's
  survivor's light

Peter Weltner taught English Renaissance poetry and prose and modern and contemporary British, Irish, and American fiction and poetry at San Francisco State for thirty seven years. He has published twenty books or chapbooks of fiction or poetry including most recently *The Return of What's Been Lost*, *The Light of the Sun Become Sea*, and *You Wait For Me Where Mountain Peaks Are White As Your Hair*. He lives with his husband in San Francisco by the Pacific.

www.ingramcontent.com/pod-product-compliance
Lightning Source LLC
Chambersburg PA
CBHW030748110726
47900CB00008B/2499